Susanna Don't You Cry

a novel

Zachary McIntire

based on a story by
Rachael McIntire

ISBN 978-0692435472

Visit elishapress.com for a free digital
version of this book and other titles.

Table of Contents

1

Strike Out

Chuck Kincaid was eleven years old, and already in love – with baseball, that is. His '81 World Series cap was already tattered and faded, but still it hardly left his head from morning until night. His mother forbade him to bring his bat to the dinner table, so he settled for keeping his glove under his chair. That way it was readily available for a game of catch, just as soon as he could wolf down his supper.

Chuck's dad, Ross, used to join him outside for half an hour or so, but the last few months he had been too busy. So Chuck proceeded to teach his little sister, Kelly, how to handle the bat, ball, and glove properly.

Though only six, Kelly was a willing student, and demonstrated an unusual degree of athletic prowess for her age. Summer days found the two perfecting some aspect of the game out in the backyard for hours at a time.

"I need a sip!" gasped Kelly one afternoon after Chuck had drilled her on running the bases.

"You always need a *sip*!" Chuck complained, but relented, since he himself had worked up quite a sweat. They had their traditional race to the back porch, and Chuck, having won, jerked open the screen door, only to observe his dad and mom standing in the kitchen, obviously in the middle of an argument.

Kelly came charging in after him, but immediately stepped back and hid behind her big brother. Their parents had been arguing a lot lately, but usually behind closed doors. Sometimes their dad would storm out of the house, threatening to fly off in his plane and disappear. He always came back in a better mood, though, and sometimes even apologized. But both Kelly and Chuck instinctively knew that this time was different.

"It's no use, Susanna, I'm leaving!" Ross was heatedly asserting, when the children burst in.

"But Ross, you can't just break up our home," Susanna pleaded. "The children need you, and... I need you!" She collapsed in a kitchen chair, her head buried in her hands, weeping uncontrollably.

"I'm sure you'll find someone else to *need* after I'm gone," Ross replied, obviously unmoved by her pitiful outburst. "Hopefully it will be someone who doesn't mind you hanging on him twenty-four hours a day."

"In the meantime," he continued, "I intend to start a new life. You'll be hearing from my lawyer, but I'm not interested in the house, or the cars, or custody of...." The list trailed off as he noticed the last two items on it, standing in the doorway.

Chuck reeled at the impact of what was happening. He had privately wondered for a while if his parents were headed toward divorce, but he'd never imagined it happening like this. If his dad wasn't interested in custody, it had to mean that he not only didn't want to be married, he didn't want his children, either.

"Dad, you... you can't be serious!" Chuck stammered.

Ross ignored the question, as if answering it might make him change his mind. Then, picking up his suitcase, he headed for the front door.

Kelly followed close behind him, crying and shaking; she hadn't understood all the words, but her heart had gotten the picture. She reached out and clung to her father's waist.

"Daddy... please don't leave us... *please*!" she sobbed.

Ross didn't even look down, but just disengaged Kelly's little arms firmly, and not too gently from his body, and walked out of the house.

Chuck watched through the window as his dad headed for a baby-blue sports coupe that was parked across the street. He recognized the driver: it was his dad's personal assistant, Colleen Spears. Everything made sense – in a horrible sort of way – as Chuck saw his dad climb into the car, and greet his platinum-blonde secretary with an affectionate peck on the cheek.

Chuck became a man in that moment, his childish innocence and trust shattered by that single scene, imprinted bitterly and indelibly in his memory.

I'll never forgive him – never! Chuck promised himself, as he reached his arms out to enfold the crying Kelly. Aloud, he said consolingly, "It's all right, Babe." (She was Babe and he was Lou on the

ball field.) "Mom and I will take good care of you."
Kelly sniffled and tried to be brave. "Won't we,
mom?" Chuck continued, and looked around at his
mother.

Susanna turned swollen eyes toward her pitiful
little family. "Sure, honey," she whispered hoarsely,
and thrust her head back into the wet cradle of her
arms.

Chuck cast a helpless glance at his heartbroken
mother, and made up his mind right then that getting
her and Kelly through this ordeal was going to be a
one-man job. He walked softly toward his mother and
encircled her heaving shoulders with a still short,
pudgy arm. Then, with uncharacteristic affection, he
kissed her cheek.

"Mom, I'm taking Kelly outside. Will you be all
right?" Susanna nodded silently.

Chuck turned sadly, took Kelly's hand, and went
back out into the yard. The sun was still shining, and
the birds were still singing. Nothing had changed –
and yet nothing would ever be the same.

Chuck and Kelly batted and pitched themselves
into exhaustion that afternoon. Finally, stretching out
under the huge, friendly oak tree in the backyard, they
lay on their backs staring blankly into the sky.

"Chuck, where did Daddy go?" Kelly finally
asked, with childish innocence.

"Don't know, and don't care," answered Chuck
bitterly.

"You suppose he'll come back home tonight?"
she asked hopefully, her big blue eyes glistening.

"No, Kelly," he replied solemnly, "he's not *ever* coming back. Just forget him. He's no good."

"But I love Daddy, Chuck," said Kelly, confused and hurt that her brother should suddenly talk about Daddy that way.

"I don't, Kelly. Not anymore. I hate him. Don't ever mention his name to me again, you understand?" Chuck jumped up, hurled a rock as far as he could toward the back woods, and then ran into the house. Kelly followed him, because she had no one else to follow.

2

The Loser

Even after she had signed the divorce papers, Susanna couldn't make herself believe that she wasn't somehow stuck in a nightmare. But when she saw the picture of a smiling Ross and Colleen in the wedding announcements, reality finally sank in: he was gone for good.

Chuck heard his mother crying, and came into the kitchen, with Kelly trailing close behind. He picked up the paper she'd thrown in the floor, took one look at the picture, and stuffed the whole thing angrily in the trash can.

"You're better off, Mom," he declared, trying desperately to make his little boy's voice sound more like a man's. "If Daddy was mean enough to do what he did to you, Colleen Spears is getting just what she deserves – *him*!" Then, not knowing what else to say, the children left their mother weeping once more at the kitchen table, and ran outside to play another bitter game of catch.

If they had looked up into the sky at the right time that afternoon, they might have noticed a small private plane winging its way toward Colorado. At its controls was their father: flying high both literally and figuratively. The euphoria he felt at that moment had almost completely anesthetized his conscience. No more moody wife, no more whining kids; just Ross

Kincaid and the girl of his dreams, soaring through the clouds to a new life together.

Later that evening, as dusk gathered over the Rocky Mountains, ominous weather reports coming over the radio began to intrude on their perfect picture.

"What's the matter, honey?" Colleen asked, noting his furrowed brow.

"Heavy storms moving in over Denver," he translated. "They're rerouting some of the commercial flights."

"Oh no," she moaned, "don't tell me we're going to have to spend our wedding night at some second-rate motel in the middle of nowhere!"

"I hope not, baby. Right now it's just an advisory for private planes, but I sure don't like the look of those clouds."

"And our special table at Roberto's!" she suddenly remembered, ignoring his concern. "I won't be able to get that reservation again before we have to leave. Oh, Ross, we just have to make it into Denver tonight."

Glancing again at his charts, Ross calculated the risks. An experienced pilot, he knew better than to disregard a weather advisory without a really good reason. But at just that moment, the charming, persuasive woman in the seat next to him seemed like a very compelling reason. He would do just about anything to make her happy.

"Don't worry, sweetheart," he assured her. "I'll get us there on time."

The confident smile she flashed back at him made Ross feel that he could land a jumbo jet on a baseball diamond. But twenty minutes later, on the final approach, he began to realize he'd made the wrong decision.

"Eight niner bravo, advise you abort this landing and head over to Boulder. Ground level winds are unpredictable, gusting to four zero knots."

Ross tightened his grip on the controls and tried not to let the rising fear creep into his voice. "Negative; insufficient fuel remaining. I need to make this work."

There was a slight pause. Ross knew what it meant; they didn't want to let him land under those conditions, but he'd left them no choice.

"Roger, eight niner bravo, continue approach."

As the runway lights appeared through the rain, Ross began to feel the small craft bucking and rolling in the violent winds. *God, help me...,* he started to pray, but caught himself. There was no doubt in his mind that he had left God, along with his family, back in California.

That was the last thought he had before a vicious gust caught the Cessna broadside, and Ross felt himself lose control. He heard Colleen scream as the starboard wingtip slammed into the ground, and then the whole world spun and crashed into blackness.

The next thing Ross heard was a voice, very far away, calling his name.

"Mr. Kincaid? Mr. Kincaid, can you hear me? If you can hear me, lift your right hand."

Ross tried to open his eyes, but found he couldn't. He then tried his voice, but all that came out was a muffled groan. Finally, he just did as instructed and raised his hand a few inches – and felt intense waves of pain radiate through his back and shoulder.

"That's fine, Mr. Kincaid," said the voice, "just lie still now. You've been in a serious plane crash, but you're going to be all right."

Ross tried to speak again. "My eyes," he croaked, "why can't I open them?"

"There are bandages on your face, but don't worry, your eyes are just fine."

The memory of the crash was beginning to return – the runway lights, the storm, Colleen's scream....

"My wife!" He tried to sit up, but both the nurses and the pain quickly returned him to his pillow. "Is Colleen okay?"

The silence of the hospital staff answered his question. Colleen was gone. The woman he gave up everything for, the one he was going to start a new life with... gone. All their plans and dreams lay in a mass of smoldering, twisted metal on an airport tarmac. Why hadn't he died, too? What was there left to live for?

"Mr. Kincaid, is there anyone in your family we should contact?"

"I... have no family," Ross replied, feeling the crushing weight of loneliness in those words. An only child with both parents long dead, Ross literally had no one in the world to turn to. All he had was money, which, as he soon discovered, made a very poor substitute during a long and painful recovery.

In addition to many other injuries, his face had been severely burned in the crash, and required multiple reconstructive surgeries. The doctors did their best, but the face they created hardly resembled the handsome profile that Ross, in his younger days, had often secretly admired.

After his eventual release from the hospital, Ross decided he couldn't face returning to California. He took a job with a company in New York, which proved to be the first of many aimless stops on a quest to rebuild his mangled life. Some of the scars on his body faded with time, but not the scars on his soul.

3
Man Of The House

The newspaper at the Kincaid home was rain-soaked the evening the article came out about the plane crash. Susanna heard a few sketchy details months later from a friend, but she said nothing to the kids. There was no use arousing Kelly's hopes, or Chuck's anger. Not being a vengeful person herself, she took no satisfaction in the news of Colleen's death. Although she didn't learn the extent of Ross's injuries, she knew he was alive. It hurt all over again to realize that, even without Colleen, he didn't want her back.

As for Chuck and Kelly, they were making the best they could out of the shattered pieces of their lives. They grew up quickly – too quickly. Ross had left Kelly at an age when little girls would normally play dolls every waking hour. But Kelly had no desire to make believe about a pretend family; her own family situation was too painful for her to want to emulate. So she contented herself with being Chuck's ever-faithful sidekick.

In time, she stopped even mentioning her daddy; she learned it made her mommy cry, and her brother would just walk away. But Chuck did not forget his father. Childish anger hardened into genuine hate as time passed. Chuck vowed to himself again and again, *I'll never forgive him.*

As promised, Susanna got the house, cars, and sole custody of the children in the divorce, but Ross's high-powered lawyer had maneuvered her into giving up alimony in exchange. Fortunately, she had a teaching degree to fall back on, and the high school where she had worked before she married Ross was happy to hire her back. So, Chuck was left to look after Kelly, and Kelly was left to look up to Chuck.

Even after five years had passed, when most boys would consider an eleven-year-old kid sister a pest, Chuck included Kelly in all his plans. He taught her how to play ball as well as any boy, and they spent hours watching the Dodgers on TV, or admiring their huge baseball card collection.

When Chuck got a part-time job after school at a local burger joint, Kelly would get her school bus driver to drop her off nearby. She would sit in the corner booth and do her homework or read until Chuck got off work at six. Then they would chug on home in the '73 VW bug Chuck was paying for by the month with his earnings – and holding together with generous applications of duct tape. Susanna arrived as late as they did, as she had made a habit of stopping by the local singles bar for a cocktail before heading home.

Susanna had tried the whole first year after the divorce to be both mother and father to her children. But as time went on, she found herself leaning more on Chuck for moral support – and more on drink to escape the loneliness and rejection that were slowly eating away at her soul.

Since Chuck was already becoming a substitute father to his little sister, his mother's growing dependence on him fit in with the role he was gradually assuming. It was not unusual, when they all got home at the same time, for Chuck to take the lead in deciding where they would go for supper. Susanna could no longer motivate herself to cook, and Chuck and Kelly had always preferred baseball to dishes anyway.

Ten years passed for the orphaned Kincaid family. Susanna no longer stopped for just one drink at the singles bar: she stayed every evening until closing time. Chuck had shouldered a good portion of the burden of family support, having traded his childhood dream of becoming a doctor for auto mechanic's classes in high school. There was no money for college now – another reason to hate the man who had wrecked his life.

At sixteen, Kelly had finally outgrown both baseball and brotherly advice, and was busy taking advantage of her mostly parentless existence. Chuck worked long hours, and rarely found time to rebuke his headstrong sister for staying out late, or for "borrowing" money from his wallet. His mother had her own sad world of liquor and – Chuck suspected – drugs. Her pocketbook had fallen from the kitchen table one afternoon, and to his horror, Chuck had seen eight or ten different prescription bottles rolling over the floor.

"Mom, what's all this?" he demanded, obviously distraught.

"Oh, darling, it's nothing," Susanna lied. "My doctor says my nerves are bad. He just gives me a little something to help me sleep."

If those are sleeping pills, Chuck thought, *then why do you carry them in your pocketbook?* He just helped her gather up the bottles, though, and said nothing more. Chuck loved his mother, and if she had problems... well, he knew who was to blame for that.

4
Jacob

The years had been no kinder to the absent father of the Kincaid home. Seven different jobs in four states had filled his bank account nicely, but not the void in his heart and soul. Finally realizing that changes of scenery weren't helping, he settled down in Texas. And, for lack of anything meaningful to do with his life, he made more money.

The commercial construction business was like a huge game of Monopoly, except it was played with real cash, and a lot of big bank loans. It was, at times, quite exciting, and being in the thick of it was the closest Ross ever came to happiness anymore. He managed not to think about anything but work during the daylight hours, which was pretty easy for a man who literally never took a day off. But the long, quiet nights were a different story. Memories would return whether he wanted them to or not: the quaint little coffee shop where he proposed to Susanna; their wedding on the beach at Malibu; the day she told him they were going to have a baby.

But after the kids, it was like she changed into a different woman. She worried about everything, cried for no reason at all, and pestered him to death to get rid of his plane. Finally, she began having jealous fantasies, and accusing him of unfaithfulness long before he met Colleen. What began as a storybook romance had turned into the plot of a bad soap opera, like the ones Susanna seemed to watch all day long.

And then, lightning struck the second time. Colleen was everything Susanna used to be: young, fun-loving, and optimistic. For just a few magical days, it seemed he had everything he ever wanted – but again, fate said no. Somehow, it seemed he was destined to fail at everything except business, so he simply let business become his whole life.

Late one night at the office, long after every one else had gone home, Ross was poring over a set of prints at his desk. The bid wasn't due for three weeks, but it was as good a reason as any to delay going home with himself. He had just started the concrete calculations, when his concentration was interrupted by the sound of someone whistling out in the hall. From a long-buried corner of his memory came the words to the tune: *Jesus loves the little children, all the children of the world.*

Ross had first learned that song when he was seven – the same year his father died in a construction accident. People in the church said it would be all right, because he was with Jesus. *But if Jesus loves me*, he had thought as he sat in Sunday school, *then why did He take my daddy away?*

His mother never seemed troubled by that sort of question. She was a simple woman with a simple faith that sustained her, first through her husband's death, and then through her own losing battle with cancer, twelve years later. For Ross, though, faith just wasn't enough. He had no particular use for God, and by now he was quite sure that if God existed, the feeling was mutual.

Still, whether from a sense of nostalgia, or just idle curiosity, Ross suddenly wanted to know who it was that still remembered that old song. He opened his office door and peered around it to find a small, wiry man pushing a floor mop. He looked to be about thirty-five, with dark hair and a neatly trimmed beard. On his carefully pressed uniform shirt was a name tag that read "Jacob." Somehow, he didn't strike Ross as a typical janitor: his face looked too intelligent and – strangely – happy.

Ross realized he was staring about the same time Jacob did. "Oh, Mr. Kincaid," he apologized, "I didn't realize you were still here. Sorry if I bothered you."

Ross was taken aback. "How do you know my name?" he asked bluntly.

"It's on your office door," Jacob replied simply. "I usually get here a bit earlier, and I've seen you quite a few times. Seems like you're always the last to leave."

"That's true enough," Ross agreed.

"You must really love your work," Jacob offered.

"I wouldn't call it 'love'," Ross snorted. "It fills up the days, but it sure doesn't make me whistle down the hall."

Jacob smiled. "Well, it's not my work that makes me whistle, either."

"Well, what is it then?" The question was a reflex that Ross immediately regretted, knowing the kind of answer he would get.

"The goodness of God," Jacob replied, in as matter-of-fact a tone as he might use to give the time.

"The goodness of God." Ross repeated the phrase flatly. "Is that what you call this rat race?"

"No," Jacob mused, leaning on his mop handle. "I think that's called 'life.' But God's goodness is what makes the rat race bearable. Everywhere I look, I see it."

"That's some pair of rose-colored glasses you've got there, buddy," Ross retorted.

Jacob looked puzzled as he took off his glasses and inspected them carefully. "No, that's just the floor cleaner," he explained solemnly.

Ross gave the janitor a strange look, then caught the facetious twinkle in his eye, and they laughed together. Ross hadn't laughed with anyone in a long time, and it felt good. "I didn't mean to give you a hard time," he said apologetically. "I'm glad you enjoy your life, and it's certainly not your fault that mine stinks."

"Everybody's life stinks without God, Mr. Kincaid. Some people just don't realize it. Before I met Jesus, I thought I was a pretty good person."

"Which you probably were," Ross surmised.

Jacob shook his head. "Oh, I made sure it looked that way to others: I ate kosher, studied Torah and Talmud, and never missed synagogue. But inside, my heart was full of lust and pride, and I eventually caused other people to suffer as a result of my choices. In short, I was *not* a good person."

Ross yawned deliberately. "Yeah, well, we all make mistakes," he said. "And I'm going to be making plenty of them tomorrow if I don't get home and get some sleep. Nice talking to you, Jacob."

Jacob, though he obviously wasn't buying Ross's transparent exit ploy, was unperturbed. "Good night, Mr. Kincaid," he said. "I hope we'll get a chance to talk again soon."

Well, that makes one of us, Ross thought.

"Call me Ross," he said instead. "Nobody calls me 'Mr. Kincaid' but people who want to sell me something."

"Well, that wouldn't include me," Jacob smiled. "The only thing I have worth selling is free."

Ross stepped out into the chilly evening, wondering why he felt like running from a janitor. He was obviously a harmless religious nut.

Well, in order to be happy, you have to be crazy, Ross thought as he climbed into his truck. *I guess I'm better off miserable.*

5
Found

Susanna dragged her weakened body out of bed and made herself get ready for school. Each day it grew harder to do her job. So many papers to grade, parents to see, meetings to attend. How much longer could she go on?

Shakily, but with tenderness, she picked up the little music box, made in the shape of a banjo, which had been Ross's present to her on their first wedding anniversary. She wound up the key, and listened to the tune it played, *Oh Susanna, Don't You Cry.* The irony was that she nearly always cried when she heard it, yet it also brought her some solace in her pain to remember a time in her life when she was loved. It seemed to give her just enough motivation for one more teaching day.

In the bathroom, a cocktail of pills was waiting that her body now seemed to require, just to stay upright and mobile. Having supplemented these with her "breakfast," which consisted of several cups of strong coffee, she stepped out into the biting wind to face a cold, indifferent world again.

Chuck, as usual, had warmed up her car before leaving for work himself ten minutes earlier. *Dear Chuck,* Susanna thought. *He's always trying to make it up to me.* She arrived at school glassy-eyed and nervous, but determined to keep up the act as long as she could. She reached into her teacher's mailbox and found a simple message: *Mrs. Kincaid, please come to my office directly after school – Mr. Tyler.*

    Probably Ronny's dad complaining about too little homework, she mentally guessed. But the vague apprehension Susanna had felt as she read the note, gradually turned into dread as the day dragged on. Finally – last bell. She freshened her lipstick and strode down the corridors to Mr. Tyler's office, as if her stride would produce a confidence she did not feel.

    "Come in, Mrs. Kincaid," Mr. Tyler directed. "Sit down, please. I'll get straight to the point, although I wish this meeting were not necessary."

    The soft-spoken principal could have stopped right there; Susanna knew what was coming. But he cleared his throat and went on.

    "You've been back with us for just over ten years. You were rehired initially on your excellent reputation as a high school history teacher a number of years before. But your performance the second time around, I'm sorry to say, has gradually deteriorated into all but non-performance.

    "I have here a test taken by one of the better students in your class. You had his paper marked with five incorrect answers. It has *none*. He tells me this is the norm, not only with his papers, but with other students' papers as well. He also reported – without rancor, I might add – that on many occasions your instructions in the classroom are somewhat less than coherent.

"This is not the first such report I have received, Mrs. Kincaid, but I trust it will be the last. I have tried to be understanding of the strain you have endured as a… uh... single parent, but life must go on. And my first priority, as I'm sure you realize, must be the quality of teaching in the school."

He seemed to be looking for some reaction, so Susanna nodded mechanically.

"With the approval of the superintendent," he continued, "I am placing you on three months' probation. During that time, if you are able to... uh... work out these issues, we will be happy for you to remain in your post. Otherwise, we shall have to ask for your resignation."

He stopped, seeming to search for some expression of his powerless sympathy. "I know these are hard words, Mrs. Kincaid," he said, "but I mean them kindly. I hope you understand."

"Yes, Mr. Tyler, I do. Thank you." There was nothing else to say, and Susanna hadn't the strength to utter another syllable. But once inside the haven of her car, she came apart completely. She wept uncontrollably: for herself, for her children, for the mess she had made of her life. Others with her circumstances had made the best of a bad deal, but she had chosen escape – any escape – and now it had caught up with her.

"God, where are you? I need help!" she screamed in desperation.

Do you really think God is listening to you? whispered a voice inside her head. *You're too far gone*

for anyone to help. Why don't you just end it all?
Susanna drove to a nearby mall to walk and to think.
She had heard that voice before, but this was the first
time she had ever seriously considered heeding it.

She walked the mall aimlessly for what seemed
like hours until, exhausted, she looked for a place to sit
down where no one would see her or try to talk to her.
A four-feature theater seemed like as good a place as
any, so she bought a ticket to a random movie, without
even looking at the title. Emotionally and physically
spent, she collapsed into a seat near the back. She sat
there for a long time, not really seeing or hearing
anything – just wishing the whole world would
disappear. *There are plenty of pills in your purse,* the
voice suggested. *Just go home, go to sleep, and don't
wake up.*

It was hard to believe how alluring the prospect
seemed. Chuck and Kelly would understand – and
they'd be better off without her. She could just go
home, go to bed, and....

"Come unto me all ye that labor, and are heavy
laden, and I will give you rest."

Startled, Susanna looked up. She had not heard
one word of the movie that was playing until that
point. But now, it seemed as though the man on the
screen was speaking directly to her. And suddenly she
was listening, thinking that those words were some of
the sweetest she had ever heard. As she soon figured
out, the film was about the life of Jesus.

Susanna's parents had been Christmas and Easter
churchgoers. They had sent her to Sunday school for a

while, but didn't complain when she quit going in the
sixth grade. She had never paid much attention to
anything in church but the boys, anyway. Stories out
of a book written two thousand years ago just never
seemed that relevant to her life.

Now, as she watched, she learned of a Jesus she
never knew. Of a savior who accepted outcasts,
forgave sinners, and put broken lives back together.
Of a king who let his enemies nail him to a cross – and
then prayed for their forgiveness with his dying breath.
Could it really be true that he rose from the dead?
Could this be God's answer to her desperate cry for
help?

*But what am I supposed to do? Where do I find
Him?*

It wasn't exactly a prayer, but she got what
looked like an answer anyway, in the form of a picture
that suddenly sprang into her mind. It was of a little
mission for alcoholics and homeless people, just a few
blocks from the mall. In happier times, Susanna used
to volunteer there occasionally, sorting clothes and
other donations. She never talked much to the couple
that ran it, but she knew they were real Christians. If
anyone could help her....

Now you really are cracking up, the mocking
voice said. *You're going to go crawling into that
mission like some derelict, begging for soup, soap and
salvation?*

Susanna had started to get up, but now she
hesitated. And then came another voice: calmer,

quieter, and much more sensible. *What do you have to lose?*

Within a few minutes, Susanna was climbing the narrow stone steps to the front door of the mission. But her heart sank when she realized that the sign was gone and the windows were dark. Like everything else in her life, it was a dead-end road.

"Oh, don't tell me they're closed?" Once again, a voice startled Susanna. But this time, she turned to find it belonged to a woman, a little shorter and younger than herself, standing just behind her on the steps. Her round face was flushed from exertion, and her arms overloaded with an enormous pile of old clothes and blankets.

"I couldn't find a parking space any closer than three blocks," she moaned. "I had no idea they weren't here anymore."

Instincts took over that had nothing to do with Susanna's current frame of mind. "Here, let me help you with some of that," she offered.

"Oh, you are so sweet," said the stranger appreciatively, letting her take a few coats and a patchwork quilt. "Did you come here to bring donations too?"

"Not exactly," Susanna blushed. "I used to volunteer here, though – a long time ago."

"Really? So did I! Right before my last baby came. I'm Tina Pillow, by the way."

"Susanna Kincaid – nice to meet you."

As they walked back to her car, Tina chattered pleasantly about a variety of subjects. Susanna mostly just listened, wondering how she got from contemplating suicide to holding a normal conversation.

When the donations were safely stowed away in the back of her minivan, Tina took Susanna's hand warmly. "Thank you so much for your help. Can I buy you a cup of coffee?"

Susanna found herself accepting the offer without even thinking. There was something in this woman that she felt drawn to; it was almost like unexpectedly meeting an old friend in the middle of a strange city. The coffee shop, too, was a warm and inviting little nook, with a young man playing his guitar on a small stage, and singing softly.

"I love this place," Tina confided. "My husband and I come here whenever we can get away for an hour or so. It's a great spot to just sit and enjoy each other's company."

In spite of her determination to hold herself together, tears welled up from Susanna eyes and rolled down her cheeks. She tried to hide them by sipping her coffee, but her hand shook so badly she had to put the cup back down.

"Why Susanna," Tina asked tenderly, "what ever is the matter?"

"I'm so sorry," Susanna said, dabbing her eyes with a paper napkin. "My husband proposed to me in a coffee shop many years ago." She hesitated a moment, then added, "My ex-husband, that is."

Tina's voice was soft with genuine concern. "Would you like to talk about it?"

In ten years, Susanna had never confided to her closest friends what was really going on in her life, let alone a total stranger. But now, it was as though a crack had opened in the levee around her heart, and an ocean of sorrow spilled out. She told Tina everything: from the divorce, to the alcohol and drugs, to the impending loss of her job and the voice that had told her to end it all. Her new friend listened, and cried with her, but through her tears, her face seemed to glow.

"And then," Susanna finished, "I saw Jesus on the screen, saying, 'Come to me, and I will give you rest.' That's why I really went to the mission tonight – I was trying to find Him."

"Susanna, I have some great news for you." Tina's voice was hoarse with tears, yet she seemed almost bursting with happiness. "It was God's Holy Spirit who sent you to that mission, just like He sent me. He meant for us to meet, so you could meet Jesus."

As Tina frankly and simply explained the Gospel, Susanna felt her heart taking hold, as though the words were a life ring that would keep her from drowning. Years of sorrow and rejection were swept away by an overwhelming, unconditional love, pouring out of a cross where God's Son had given his life for her. At the foot of that cross she laid the tattered remains of her life, and asked Jesus Christ to be her Savior.

Somewhere within Heaven's portals that night, the angels thrilled to the Good Shepherd's cry:

"Rejoice with me, for I have found my sheep, which was lost."

6

Second Chances

Chuck grew fidgety as the clock struck ten. Mom had never been this late, and Kelly wasn't home yet either. A whimsical sticky note on the fridge explained, "Doing homework with Samantha. Home by nine."

But Chuck knew his little sister too well to believe that whopper. It was he who had forged signatures on Kelly's report cards to save Mom the heartbreak of Kelly's failures at school. Barring some miracle, Kelly would remain a junior next year. How much longer could he hide the truth from his mother?

Kelly wasn't going to change, either. She seemed determined to wreck her life before it even got started, and nothing Chuck tried seemed to help. Despite her natural athletic ability, and her brother's patient coaching, she never lasted long on a sports team. If she wasn't on academic probation, then she was skipping practices to meet up with some long-haired, brainless boyfriend, a species she seemed to have made a hobby of collecting.

Time was when the kids in Kelly's class would have been a better influence on her, Chuck reflected. But both their neighborhood, and the school Kelly attended, had been in slow decline for several years. The kind of kids she now had for friends, seemed more likely to have their faces in a police mug book than in their senior yearbook. Kelly herself had been caught with marijuana twice now – both times insisting it belonged to someone else – and Chuck worried himself to death wondering what kind of stunt she was going to pull next.

The sound of his mother's car pulling into the garage brought Chuck's thoughts back to the present. "Mom, where have you been?" he reproached her anxiously as she came in.

"Oh, Chuck, I'm so sorry. I wouldn't have had you worried like this for anything.   Something... amazing has happened to me tonight. I have to tell you and... wait, has Kelly gone to bed already?" Susanna had only just noticed that her daughter's usual spot in front of the TV was empty.

"She's not home yet," Chuck answered, too worried to try to cover for Kelly. "The note she left said she'd be back by nine o'clock. I'm afraid that sister of mine is going to give me gray hair before I'm thirty! But what's your news, Mom? You look… well… happy for a change."

Before Susanna could reply, the phone rang. Late-night phone calls when any of her family was out had always made Susanna anxious, and the worry on Chuck's face only added to her own as she picked up the receiver.

"Hello?"

"Is this Mrs. Kincaid of 34 Grandin Place?"

"Yes, it is. Who's calling please?"

"Mrs. Kincaid, this is Lieutenant Pierce with the police department. It's about your daughter, Kelly."

Susanna felt her heart go into her throat. "Is she hurt?" she asked, fearing the worst.

"No ma'am, mostly she's just shaken up. She was in a pretty bad car wreck, but amazingly, she walked away with just a few cuts and bruises. I'm afraid one of her friends was killed, though, and there were drugs involved. We'd like you to come down to the station right away, if you can."

"We're on our way." Susanna hung up the phone and grabbed the coat she'd just taken off. Emotions of shock, sorrow, and relief collided in her heart, but she had no time to process any of them. She relayed the police officer's scant report to Chuck on the way to the station, and noticed he didn't seem surprised to learn of Kelly's involvement with drugs. *I wonder what else I don't know about my own children,* she mused. *Lord, how am I ever going to make things right?*

The waiting room at the police station was overflowing with parents, teenagers, and detectives. They didn't have to look for Kelly, though: she ran into her mother's arms, trembling and crying. Susanna suddenly realized she hadn't held Kelly close in years. She'd had no comfort to offer either of her children, but thank God, things were different tonight.

"Let's sit over here, honey," Susanna said, as she gently guided her child into a quiet corner. Kelly sat gripping her mother's hands tightly as she unburdened the horror of the hours before.

"I went to a party at Robby Crawford's house, Mom." She said it like a confession, but Susanna was ashamed that the name meant nothing to her. She gave Chuck a questioning look.

"He's a drug dealer," he said, with barely suppressed anger. "And I told you a thousand times.... Oh, what's the use?"

"I didn't know he was dealing!" Kelly protested tearfully. "Well... maybe I did know, but he seemed so nice. He was always nice to me, anyway. We had been seeing each other for a few weeks, and I thought we were going steady. He danced with me at the party; everybody was taking uppers and feeling really good. But then Robby showed us the heroin."

Susanna swallowed her shock.

"He wanted us all to shoot the stuff – he said we'd get the best high ever. But you know how much I hate needles. I told Robby I would just sniff a little, but he said I was chicken. That's why he let Samantha ride with him up front, instead of me – and she's dead, Mom! Samantha's dead!"

Kelly broke down in tears and buried her face in her mother's arms. Susanna just held her, stroking her hair, gently rocking her baby like she had so many years ago. One of the detectives standing nearby filled in the rest of the story.

"Robby Crawford took everyone for a joy ride in his parents' car," he explained. "We think he was doing around ninety-five miles an hour when he went off the road and hit a tree. The main impact was on the front passenger side, and unfortunately, Samantha Rawlings was instantly killed."

"It could have been me!" Kelly kept sobbing over and over.

"Thank God for his mercy," Susanna whispered.

Chuck gave his mother a strange look. She had never even mentioned God before, that he could recall. His dad used to, occasionally, but only when he cursed. *It's all his fault*, Chuck thought, as the memory of his father stirred up his anger once again. *Kelly has practically had to raise herself, and it's thanks to him that we're stuck in this lousy neighborhood. If he'd stuck around and done his job, none of this would have happened.*

Susanna turned to the detective. "What happens now?"

The young man stepped aside for a brief consultation with his lieutenant.

"We're not going to charge your daughter this time, Mrs. Kincaid," he said when he returned. "But I hope this tragedy will serve as a wake-up call. Not everyone gets a second chance."

"Thank you, officer," Susanna said sincerely. *Thank you, Jesus,* she thought. "Come on, Chuck, let's take Kelly home."

7
A Cup Of Cold Water

Ross snuffed out the last of his cigarette in the already-full ashtray and lit another. For once, he actually had a good reason for working late: his *former* assistant had completely messed up a change order that was due to be presented to the city council the next morning. Ross had been about ready to fire the guy anyway; a few drinks at the office party was one thing, but keeping a bottle of gin in your desk drawer was another.

Despite the loneliness of his existence, Ross had promised himself that he'd never try to dull the pain with drugs, alcohol, or religion. He might not be the man he once was, but he'd never reach for a crutch – he'd stand on his own two feet until the day they carried him out in a box. Realizing his coffee was cold, Ross got up to get a refill – and heard a loud crash outside his office door.

Rushing into the hall, he found Jacob sprawled awkwardly on top of a fallen ladder.

"Are you okay?" Ross asked with alarm. "Should I call an ambulance?"

Still a bit dazed, Jacob shook his head. "No, thanks, I'll be fine. I was just trying to change that filter...." He indicated a grille high up on the wall.

Ross helped Jacob to his feet and set the ladder back up. "Are you sure you can manage?"

"Oh, I think so," Jacob said, but his first wobbly step up the ladder proved him obviously wrong.

"Forget about it, pal," Ross said as helped him down. "You're in no shape to be climbing ladders. I think you'd better go home."

"Maybe you're right," Jacob agreed. "Can you help me find my glasses?"

"Uh...," Ross hesitated, "you're wearing them?"

Jacob chuckled at himself. "I guess my vision's a little blurry tonight. I'll just take the bus home."

"No you won't either," Ross said firmly. "There's three streets between here and the bus stop, and you're bound to get yourself run over. I'll drive you home – where do you live?"

"It's way on the other side of town," Jacob protested. "If you can just get me to the bus stop...."

"Where I should be taking you is the hospital," Ross interrupted. "Have you seen a doctor?"

Jacob nodded. "Quite a few of them, in fact."

"And?"

Jacob was silent a few moments, and then sighed. "I have an inoperable brain tumor," he said. "They tell me I have around six months to live."

Ross was stunned into silence. "I'm sorry," he finally offered, not knowing what else to say.

"Thanks," Jacob replied, "but there's no need to be. I'm going to be with Jesus."

There it is again, Ross thought. *But it's a little different, coming from a guy who's actually dying. I guess the hope of Heaven is all he's got left.*

Twenty minutes later, they arrived at a run-down, apartment building, covered about equally in graffiti, and soot from a nearby industrial park. "Is this it?" Ross questioned.

"Home sweet home," Jacob confirmed cheerfully. It was quite clear that he couldn't safely walk unaided, so Ross helped him all the way to his apartment door.

"Won't you come inside for a few minutes?" Jacob asked.

Ross wanted to say no, but couldn't. He settled himself onto the tired sofa, while Jacob, steadier in familiar surroundings, went into the kitchen for some cheese and crackers. Not surprisingly, his home was spotlessly clean, right down to the tattered drapes and faded carpet. The drab walls were sparsely adorned with two or three pictures, a menorah, and an orange plate with an inscription that read: "Pray for the peace of Jerusalem."

"I'm used to having lunch in the middle of the night," Jacob explained as he set down the plate on the coffee table. "Help yourself if you're hungry."

"Oh, not really," Ross replied. "I am a little curious, though."

"Really? About what?"

"I gather you're Jewish...?"

"Very much so," Jacob nodded, munching on a cracker.

Ross looked puzzled. "But Jews don't worship Jesus, right?"

Jacob smiled. "Well, some Jews certainly do. The Apostles were all Jewish, and almost all the New

Testament was written by Jews. In fact, Jesus Himself was a Jew, if you recall."

"Huh," Ross reflected. "I never really thought about that. But... what do you call them... Orthodox Jews – they don't believe in Jesus."

"Sadly, that's true. But those of us who have accepted Jesus as the Messiah – which means the same thing as Christ, the Anointed One – don't cease to be Jews because we believe. I think of myself as a 'completed Jew' – or just a Jewish Christian."

Ross scratched his head. "I didn't know there was any such thing."

"Well unfortunately," Jacob said, "my family agrees with you. That's why they haven't spoken to me for the last ten years."

"You've been separated from your family for ten years?"

"From my physical family, yes. But I'm part of God's family now, and I can't ever be separated from Him."

Ross had no particular interest in God's family, but he was struck by the similarity of Jacob's situation to his own. His upscale apartment was a lot nicer, but just as empty.

"Did you have a wife and kids?" he asked.

"No," Jacob replied, and then hesitated. "Actually, I do have a child somewhere, but I wasn't married to her mother. It was before I became a believer in Jesus. I've tried many times to find them, but without success. I wish they could know how sorry I am that I left them alone in the world. But some things cannot be mended in this life, except through prayer." Jacob sighed deeply.

Ross cleared his throat, sorry he had brought up the subject. "So, was it your parents that kicked you out of the family, then?"

"Yes," Jacob nodded sadly. "They were absolutely outraged when I became a believer, and said they would never speak to me again. So far, they've kept their promise: the last words I heard from my father were when he fired me from his jewelry business."

"You were a professional jeweler?" Ross didn't hide his surprise.

"Yeah, hard to believe, right? But after I left, my father discovered there were some uncut diamonds missing from his stock. He openly accused me, and with his reputation, that basically ended any future I had in the business. Since I had never finished my college degree, I didn't really have a fallback career, so I wound up sweeping dirt instead of selling diamonds."

"I can't believe you can say that with a smile," Ross marveled. "Or that you don't hate your parents for the way they ruined your life."

"They ruined my career," Jacob corrected, "but not my life. I never really lived until I found Jesus Christ, but He gave me eternal life, and no one can take that away. As for my parents, I not only don't hate them, I still love them with all my heart." He looked over wistfully at the largest picture on his wall:

a proud Jewish father with his diminutive wife and young son.

"I pray for them every day," Jacob said softly. "I don't think Heaven could be Heaven for me if they are not there."

"Well, I wouldn't worry about that too much," Ross opined. "All roads lead to Rome, right? I mean, they shouldn't have treated you that way, but I'm sure God will understand them wanting to stick with their religion."

"I know God understands," Jacob replied, "but that doesn't change his Word. Jesus said, 'no man cometh to the Father but by me.' Either He spoke the truth or He didn't – there's no middle position."

Ross shifted uncomfortably, wishing he felt free to light up a cigarette. "Well, I'm certainly no theologian," he conceded. "I just try to do the best I can, and hope the Man Upstairs will be okay with that."

"Do you really think that's a smart approach?" Jacob asked.

"What do you mean?"

"Well, suppose a client came to you and asked you to build a ten-story office building. What's the first thing you would do?"

"I'd ask him to show me the blueprints," Ross replied automatically.

"You wouldn't just start building, do the best you can, and hope he'll be pleased?"

Ross laughed at the idea, but he had met enough Christians to know where Jacob was headed. "I guess you're going to tell me that God's blueprint is in the Bible?"

"Is that so difficult for you to believe?"

"Well, no offense, but some of those stories have always seemed a little far-fetched to me."

"Truth is stranger than fiction," Jacob said with a smile. "God will give you the faith to believe, if you want to come to Him."

"Yeah, well, I'll have to think about that," Ross lied. "In the meantime, do you have anybody to look in on you?"

"Not really," Jacob admitted, "but I should be back at work tomorrow, Lord willing. The doctors tell me these dizzy spells will come and go."

Ross pulled out his business card and scribbled a number on the back. "That's my pager," he said as he handed it to Jacob. "If you need anything, you call me, okay?"

"Thank you, Ross," Jacob said. "You may not know it, but you've given a cup of cold water to one of God's children tonight."

Ross gave him a quizzical look.

"It means you've shown kindness to someone who belongs to Jesus," Jacob explained. "He promised that anyone who does that won't lose his reward."

"Oh really?" Ross quipped. "Do I win $64,000?"

"Oh, more than that," Jacob laughed. "Much more."

8

The Good News

Susanna woke the next morning with the same peace that had flooded her soul the evening before at the coffee shop. She stepped over to Kelly's room, and looked in on her little girl, her brow still furrowed in the midst of exhausted sleep.

These next days would be hard ones for Kelly, but at least Susanna now had some answers to give her – although she still had a lot of questions herself. One of those questions popped into her mind, as out of sheer habit, she reached for one of the pill bottles on the bathroom counter. Before she could even ask, she felt the answer. *You don't need those anymore*. It was the calm voice, the one Tina had said was God's Spirit.

Susanna took a deep breath. *Okay, Lord. I'm going out on a limb. Please don't let it break.*

One by one, Susanna emptied the bottles into the commode, and flushed them out of sight.

Feeling a little shaky, but excited, Susanna went downstairs to phone the school secretary, and ask for a few days of personal leave. She could tell by the tone of Carolyn's voice that she expected the "leave" to be permanent. *I guess she's in for a surprise,* Susanna thought. *I hope.*

When Kelly woke up, it was to a smell that was very unusual in her house: the aroma of breakfast cooking. Donning her housecoat, she went downstairs and peered into the kitchen. There, clad in an apron, holding a spatula, and looking for all the world like all the happy housewives on TV, stood her mother. If everything that had happened last night seemed like a bad dream, this seemed like a good one... in a crazy sort of way.

"Good morning, sweetheart," Susanna smiled as she noticed her standing there. "I was just about to come and call you. I thought we'd have breakfast together this morning; how does that sound?"

For a moment, Kelly just stared at her, with a look that said, "Who are you and what have you done with my mother?" Then she finally managed a dumbfounded nod, and sat down. Lifting her fork over her pancakes a few moments later, Kelly got another shock when Susanna took her hand, and bowed her head.

"Dear God, thank you so much for today... that we're alive to see it, and that we have each other. And thank you, most of all, for Jesus. Amen."

"Uh, Mom," Kelly asked with almost fearful hesitation, "are you going to tell me what's going on? Is this all because of what happened last night?"

"In a way, yes," her mother replied. "But you don't know *everything* that happened last night. In fact, I don't think either you or Chuck really know everything that's been going on for the last ten years, but it's time for that to change. Are you up for a sad story with a happy ending?"

"Sure, Mom," yawned a male voice from the doorway. "But could you make it *short* and happy? I overslept, and I need to be at work in thirty minutes."

"Oh, hi, Chuck. I thought you'd gone to work already, but I'm glad you're still here."

Kelly was not sure *she* was glad, but soon forgot how she begrudged sharing the moment with her brother. Listening to the story her mother told of the last decade was like feeling the fresh air and sunshine pour through a newly opened window into a dark, stuffy room. Never had they even once discussed these things as a family – they had been like three strangers living in the same house, each engrossed in their own bitterness, fears, and heartaches.

Finally, Susanna got to the part she had been longing to tell: the events of yesterday, and how Jesus had forgiven her for her failures as a wife and mother, and for the mess she had made of her life by wallowing in self-pity. "Kids, I'm a new person. It's so simple and so wonderful – I can't believe it took me ten miserable years to finally cry out to God."

Kelly was enthralled. Any power that could give her mother back to her was worth looking into. Her own attempts to find love had ended in heartbreak – and almost in death. She was ready to try something new. But it was Chuck who spoke: six short words. "You were *not* a bad wife." Then he jumped up abruptly and headed for the door.

Susanna was temporarily taken aback at his response, but at the same time not so shocked: she knew the deep resentment Chuck harbored toward his father. But her worries about Chuck were interrupted, as Kelly threw herself into Susanna's arms. "Mom, I'm so glad you're home!"

Susanna knew what she meant, and it made her heart glad that at least one of her children seemed to understand what had happened.

"Mom," Kelly added, "This Jesus thing you've got – I want it too. What do I do?"

In a way, Susanna was more shocked than when Kelly had admitted to dating a drug dealer. She herself had been a Christian for less than twenty-four hours, and already she was being asked to explain "this Jesus thing" to someone else! Not wanting to lose the opportunity, though, she read to Kelly from a little book about the Gospel that Tina had given her the night before.

"It's for children, really," Tina had explained. "But that's okay – Jesus actually said we have to become like little children in order to enter into his kingdom."

Kelly might have been seventeen years old, but deep inside her there was a little girl who desperately wanted a daddy. This simple, childlike explanation of a heavenly Father who loved her, and a Savior who had died to bring her back to Him, was just what her heart needed to hear.

"Dear Jesus," she prayed, "please take my life like you did Mom's. Please... forgive me for all the rotten things I've done. I really want to be a part of your family. Amen."

She looked up at her mom uncertainly. "Was that okay?"

"It was more than okay," Susanna smiled tearfully. "It was beautiful."

That day was unlike any either mother or daughter had ever experienced, even before the divorce. They spent it all together, doing dishes, cleaning the house, and going to the mall to watch (and re-watch) the film about Jesus that had started Susanna on her quest the previous night.

By evening, Kelly was ready to share her "new" mother with the brother she had once idolized. Chuck, a little puzzled by the obvious change in them both, nonetheless showed no interest in the source of their newfound joy. "I'm happy for you guys," he said, "but religion is not for me. I intend to make something of myself, and God is only going to get in my way."

"You sound exactly like your dad, Chuck," Susanna blurted out without thinking. "He would never let anything stand in his way, either. And just look what it did to our family!"

Stung by her words, Chuck visibly bristled. "You don't have to remind me what Dad did to our family, Mom," he said evenly. "I have never forgotten it, and I never will." Then, with barely concealed anger, he got up and left the table.

Susanna dropped her head to her hand. "Dear Lord, why did I say that?" she whispered remorsefully.

"It's okay, Mom," Kelly tried to console her. "He'll get over it."

Susanna squeezed her daughter's hand. "I'm afraid we've both got a lot of learning to do, honey. But at least we're started down the right road together."

9
The Locker

Ross drummed his fingers impatiently on the exam table top, and glanced for the twentieth time at his watch. He was beginning to wish he'd put off his yearly physical again, like he had three times in the last month. But Charlene, the office manager, had practically shoved him out the door this time, insisting that his health insurance policy would be canceled if he didn't get it done today.

"Sorry to keep you waiting, Ross," Dr. Tobias apologized as he arrived, breathing heavily from an apparently brisk walk. "I had to go convince a patient of mine with double pneumonia not to check herself out of the hospital."

"With the service around here, I'm not surprised she tried to escape," Ross quipped. His good-natured doctor just chuckled.

"Actually, you two should get together. I think you're the only patient I have who's more stubborn than she is."

"I'll take that as a compliment. But seriously, Doc, can we make this snappy? I've got a bid deadline in ninety minutes."

"Sure," the doctor shrugged, pretending to scribble on Ross's chart. "Based on thirty-second examination, patient appears to have advanced tuberculosis, and should be held under strict quarantine for six weeks. Next!"

"Okay, okay," Ross conceded, "do what you have to. I'm probably going to get beat on that school job anyway."

"I could give you a recommendation," Dr. Tobias offered, inflating his blood pressure cuff. "Your crew did a bang-up job on this clinic. But I thought you told me you were booked solid for the next year?"

"Hey, there's always room to grow. Who wants to be number two?"

Dr. Tobias probably would have had a retort for that, but he wasn't listening. He was looking with obvious concern at his instrument, which he proceeded to re-inflate and recheck.

"Ross," he said seriously, "have you been taking the blood pressure medication I prescribed for you last year?"

"Every day," Ross lied. (He remembered it twice a week at the most.)

Dr. Tobias looked at him doubtfully. "Your blood pressure levels are well into hypertension territory. When was your last vacation? And don't just make something up," he warned, sensing the wheels turning in his patient's head. "I can check with Charlene, you know."

"Okay," Ross admitted, "it was three years ago."

"Where did you go?" the doctor pressed. "And for how long?"

"I went to Chicago for a week."

"Wasn't that the builder's association conference?"

Ross had hoped he wouldn't remember. "Yes, but I took some time off to relax." (Another lie.)

"Ross," the doctor sighed, "I can only remember a few patients who have had hypertension as bad as yours, and they all had heart attacks or strokes within six months. Several of them died."

"Well thanks a lot, Doc," Ross snorted.

"I'm not telling you that just to scare you," he added, "but I hope you will be scared enough to listen to me for a change."

"Okay, I'm listening. What do I need, another pill? Just write me a prescription."

"Here's my prescription: take a vacation. And that means no work, period, for at least two weeks. Go to Florida, or California, or Niagara Falls – just get away and relax for a while. Your company will survive being number two until you get back."

"Okay," Ross acquiesced. "I'll try to find the time this summer."

"You'd better *make* time, and right away," the doctor insisted. "Otherwise, I guarantee your next rest will be in a hospital bed, if not in your coffin."

That last warning rolled around ominously in Ross's head as he drove back to the office. After the plane crash, he had seen enough of the inside of hospitals to last a lifetime, and he sure wasn't ready to be fitted for a casket. *Though I'm not quite sure why*, he mused. *It's not like my life means that much to anyone – including me.*

With such thoughts in his mind, Ross was a little startled to see an ambulance in front of his office building. He parked hurriedly, and reached the front door just in time to open it for two EMT's with a gurney between them. Under the oxygen mask, he recognized the pale face of Jacob Wertheim.

"Did he fall again?" he asked the medics.

"Yeah," said the one in front. "But he was in bad shape to start with. Do you know how to get in touch with his family?"

"I... uh... don't think he has any."

"Are you his friend?"

Ross hesitated. "Well, sort of...."

The EMT dropped his voice as they finished loading the gurney. "He doesn't have much time. It would be nice for someone to be with him."

Without knowing exactly why he was agreeing, Ross climbed into the ambulance. As they sped through the streets of Fort Worth, he pictured himself lying on the stretcher – and wondered who would be there to ride with him, or care if he died alone.

Two hours later, installed in a private room at Ross's insistence (and expense), Jacob regained consciousness. He was very weak, and confused at first, until Ross explained what had happened and where they were.

"This is it, then," Jacob said, very calmly.

"Yes, I guess so," Ross replied. It didn't seem necessary or appropriate to lie.

"I know you've already done a lot for me," Jacob said, "but I wonder if I could ask a final favor? It's a considerable amount of trouble, but it would mean a lot to me."

"I'll do anything for you I can," Ross promised.

"I'm not leaving behind much that I care about," Jacob said, "but I want to make sure my Bible goes to my parents, in California."

"That's no problem," Ross agreed quickly.

"Wait a second," Jacob cautioned, "it's not as simple as it sounds. I need you to deliver it to them in person, and tell them what happened to me."

"You mean... they don't know about your condition?"

"I've written them several letters, but they always send them back, and whenever they hear my voice on the phone, they hang up."

Ross shook his head. "I can't believe your own parents won't even let you tell them you're dying," he said. "But of course I'll do my best to get your Bible to them."

"Thank you so much," Jacob said sincerely. "I feel sure they'll accept it from you. And please, don't make them feel bad about what they've done to me. Tell them I love them more than ever, and I want to see them in the Father's house." His voice grew hoarse, and his eyes shone with tears.

"I've written one last letter," he said, "which I hope they will read. It's inside the Bible, along with their address. You'll find them in my locker at work – the combination is three sixteen."

Ross scribbled the number on a hospital notepad, then paused, as more old memories surfaced. "You didn't pick that number at random, did you?"

"No, it's the reference for the first Scripture I learned from the New Testament: John 3:16."

"Yeah, I remember," Ross said. "My Sunday School teacher used to call it 'the Gospel in a nutshell.'"

"That's right," Jacob agreed, his voice growing weaker. "You know, Ross, God has a locker with your name on it, and that's the combination. Inside is everything you need: forgiveness, peace, hope – eternal life. But you have to open it. He won't do that for you."

Jacob lay back on the pillow and closed his eyes, his breathing now quite shallow. He began to whisper in a language Ross didn't understand, but that he guessed was Hebrew. When he began to cough, Ross picked up his cup from the bedside table and held the straw to his lips. Jacob drank, and then smiled faintly.

"A cup of cold water," he whispered. "Remember?"

"Yeah, I remember," Ross said, having a little trouble finding his own voice. "I win the jackpot, right?"

"I'll see you on the other side," Jacob said.

And with that, he was gone.

10

New Creatures

Spring is the season when dead things come to life again. Everyone is used to that little miracle, but over the last two months, the students and faculty at Alta Vista High School had witnessed a much more astounding one. Kelly and Susanna Kincaid, a wild, mouthy junior and her alcoholic teacher mother, had somehow been transformed into completely different people.

It all started that first Monday morning after the car wreck. No one had seen either Kelly or Susanna since Wednesday night. Rumors circulated that the former had been jailed and the latter sacked, neither of which would have surprised anyone very much. But the real story, as it turned out, surprised everyone.

Carl Jackson, the first of Susanna's homeroom class to arrive, breezed in the door, gave the teacher a quick glance, then pivoted right back out. "Hey, that old battle-axe of a substitute isn't here today," he announced to his classmates. "We've got a real looker instead!" He whistled appreciatively.

Gail Tucker, a bespectacled A-student, peered around the door frame, studied the teacher intently for a few seconds, then withdrew to her friends. "Guys," she whispered loudly, "you're not going to believe this, but that's not a substitute. It's Mrs. Kincaid!"

As they filed into the classroom much more quietly than usual, the rest of the class had to agree that Carl's mistake was entirely understandable. The Mrs. Kincaid they knew was a strung-out basket case who used too much makeup, wore mismatched clothes, and tied back her unkempt pony tail with a rubber band. This lovely lady with curled brown hair, wearing a fuchsia bow blouse and navy blue suit, beaming like a light bulb – well, she was almost unrecognizable.

For the first time in ten years, Susanna was able to call the roll without having to shout over the noise of the pencil sharpener. The difficulty for her today was to keep from laughing at the bewildered faces of her students, who looked as though Cleopatra had just stepped out of a history book to take charge of the class.

The morning announcements broke the atmosphere of silent astonishment, as the principal began his daily routine over the loudspeaker. The first period bell dispersed the students to the four corners of the school, bearing the strange tale of their homeroom teacher's transformation.

Throughout the day, students and faculty alike found one excuse or another to pop into Susanna's classroom and see for themselves if the rumors were true. Mr. Carney, the head football coach, was well known for staying about ninety-nine yards from any paperwork he could avoid. Nonetheless, he somehow mysteriously ran out of staples, and naturally Mrs. Kincaid's classroom (at the opposite end of the school from his office) was the obvious place to look for some.

Mrs. Summers, the typically brusque matriarch of the school cafeteria, stopped in to discuss some unclaimed quarters that were found near the vending machine. "Have you lost any change lately?" she unabashedly inquired.

"No, thanks," replied Susanna brightly. "In fact, I've found some!"

"Uh, well... good!" fumbled the elderly cook, and beat a hasty retreat to her kitchen. If the old Susanna Kincaid was an emotional wreck, at least she was easy to understand. This new one was strange... almost scary.

But if there was anything scarier than the sudden change that had come over the eleventh-grade history teacher, it was the equally sudden metamorphosis of her daughter. Everyone had expected Kelly to be a bit subdued for a while, considering that she was the only survivor of the recent car crash not either in the hospital or in jail. But, no one expected it would be long before she returned to her rebellious, flippant ways. When she approached her science teacher at the end of class, he assumed it was to ask permission to see the school counselor. It turned out that he, too, was in for a shock.

"Mr. Hudson," she began in a quiet, shaky voice, "there's something I have to tell you."

"Yes?" he replied absently, continuing to stack papers with his usual methodical neatness.

Kelly cleared her throat, obviously trying to get up the courage to continue.

"You remember that 'A' I got on your mid-term exam?"

He nodded, starting to wonder where this was going. That particular grade had surprised the whole class; he himself was suspicious about it, but couldn't prove anything.

"I cheated on the test," she blurted out. "I'm really sorry, and I hope there's some way I can make things right before the end of the year."

Mr. Hudson, like Susanna's students that morning, was speechless. He would have been less surprised if Kelly had pulled a duck-billed platypus out of her backpack.

"Well... uh... I'm sorry to hear that, of course...." he stammered. "That is... I'm glad you told me, but I'm sorry that...." He finally gave up and started over. "Why *are* you telling me this?"

"Because I got saved last week," she answered simply. "And now I have to own up to the bad things I've done, and try to fix as many as I can."

Mr. Hudson shook his head. "Kelly," he said, "I have been teaching high school science for almost thirty years, and you are the first student that has ever confessed to cheating in my class."

Kelly's face fell, but her teacher hastened to clarify. "I didn't say you were the only student who ever cheated," he said. "Many have done that, and I'm sure that most of them never got caught. But no one ever got away with it, and then turned themselves in.

Whatever 'getting saved' means, I wish every student in this school would have that experience!"

"I'm not sure I understand it all that well myself," she acknowledged. "But I knew I had to do this. I guess it means I'll fail the class?"

The teacher stroked his beard thoughtfully. "School policy requires that you receive a failing grade on the exam," he conceded, "but that doesn't necessarily mean you can't pass the class. If you're willing to work at it, I'll try to come up with some extra assignments, so you can make up ground before the finals."

Kelly's face brightened with a beautiful smile that her teacher couldn't remember ever having seen before. "Thank you so much, Mr. Hudson! I promise I'll do whatever it takes!"

Even the naturally pessimistic science teacher found himself believing that promise. And despite his customary reticence in the teacher's lounge, this was one story he couldn't resist repeating.

By the last period, hardly a student or teacher at Alta Vista High hadn't heard some version of the day's top story from the school's "oral newspaper." Editorial headlines ranged from the cynical (*Teacher Does Personal Makeover To Save Job*) to the contemptuous (*Too Dumb To Cheat: Student Fails Self With Confession*) to the totally bizarre (*Woman And Daughter Kidnapped By UFO, Replaced With Alien Doubles*).

But as the days and weeks went by, and the initial shock wore off, the genuine interest slowly grew. A few of Kelly's less wild friends, and a couple of teachers, were even persuaded to attend the baptismal service where mother and daughter publicly professed their newfound faith in Jesus. Chuck was there too, and sincerely congratulated his mother and sister. It was clear, however, that he liked his spot on the shore, and fully intended to stay dry.

11

No Return Address

"California traffic," Ross grumbled to himself as he was cut off for the fourth time in as many miles. "Hasn't changed a bit in ten years. I'm sure this is doing wonders for my blood pressure." Despite his promise to Dr. Tobias, Ross probably would have postponed his vacation forever if Jacob's last request hadn't given him another reason to take a trip to California. Ever the efficient businessman, he saw the chance to kill two birds with one stone. The route he had planned would take him through Jacob's home town on his way to Malibu, where he had a week's reservation in a beachside resort.

The closer Ross came to the Wertheims' neighborhood, the more he began to regret his promise. Here he was, a total stranger, coming to tell a couple he'd never met that their son, whom they hated, had died and left them a book they didn't believe in. It would have been hard to invent a more bizarre and awkward situation.

But even though Ross had done a few things in life he wasn't proud of, breaking his word to a dying man was a little lower than he cared to stoop. *Maybe they won't be home*, he thought hopefully as he turned onto their quiet, tree-lined street. *I could just leave it in their mailbox with a note....*

So much for that plan. There, in the front yard of an old, but immaculate two-story brick home, stood the man from Jacob's picture, trimming his hedges. He was much grayer now, and a bit stooped, but his features still held the proud, determined look of a man who would never bend on the inside.

Reluctantly, Ross parked his truck, and made his way across the well-kept lawn. *Might as well get it over with.*

"Mr. Wertheim?"

Jacob's father looked up from his work with slight surprise. "Yes?"

Ross took a deep breath. "Mr. Wertheim, my name is Ross Kincaid. I live in Fort Worth, Texas, and I... well, I recently met your son, Jacob."

Henry Wertheim's expression didn't change, but something in his eyes seemed to turn hard. "I have no son," he said.

"Yes, I know you guys had a falling out, but I need to tell you...."

"I said I have no son," Wertheim interrupted. "I am sorry if you were misinformed." Turning back to the hedge, he took a savage chop at a stubborn branch.

Ross's fuse, which was never very long to start with, had about an inch left to burn at that point. He was on the verge of flinging the Bible at the stubborn old man, when a small figure he hadn't previously noticed rose from her chair on the covered porch.

"Mr. Kincaid?"

It had to be Jacob's mother, but the years since the picture seemed to have taken a worse toll on her than her husband. Henry glared at his wife over his shoulder, and started to say something, but then changed his mind and moved on to another stand of hedges.

"Please excuse my husband," Mrs. Wertheim apologized. "He sometimes forgets his manners. Won't you come inside and sit down?"

Ross was suddenly embarrassed by the choice words that had been going through his mind just moments before. "Ah... yes... I mean, I can't stay very long, but...."

He let the sentence trail off as he stepped inside the Wertheims' quiet house. It was just the sort of place he'd have imagined Jacob growing up in: neat, clean, and conservative. From the dark leather furniture to the antique grandfather clock, the furnishings were quality without being showy. In some strange way, though, Ross felt it was less of a home than Jacob's sparse apartment had been.

"Would you like some tea, Mr. Kincaid?"

"Um... no, thanks." Ross cleared his throat nervously. "The fact is, Mrs. Wertheim, I'm afraid I have some bad news for you."

About to sit down across from him, the elderly woman paused. Her face turned noticeably pale as she sank down into the chair. "About Jacob?"

Ross nodded, looking at the carpet, and wishing he were anywhere else in the world. "I'm afraid... he... passed away a month ago."

Hannah Wertheim caught her breath with a sharp little cry, so full of unexpected grief that it must have started as a scream deep inside her. Her face fell into her hands, and her small body trembled as she struggled to maintain her composure.

"I am... so sorry," Ross offered. His unpracticed vocabulary of sympathy exhausted, he waited in silence until Hannah found her voice again.

"How did it happen?" she asked weakly.

"It was a brain tumor – he was diagnosed last year. He didn't suffer much at all."

"Thank God for that," she murmured.

"I had only known him a few weeks, but I was with him at the end." Ross hesitated, wondering how she would react to her son's last message. "He spoke of you, and your husband. He said to tell you that he loved you both more than ever, and... wanted to see you in the Father's house." Ross sort of mumbled the last part, uncomfortably.

The old woman rocked back and forth, wiping away the tears. "Oh, Jacob," she sighed softly.

Ross reached into his briefcase, and pulled out the well-worn Bible. "He asked me to give you this."

For a few moments, Hannah just stared at the book. Ross could tell she was inwardly torn – abhorring everything that book stood for, yet yearning desperately to have some piece of her son's life to hold. Slowly, she reached out, and her fingertips touched the frayed leather edge.

"Hannah, what are you doing?!" At the angry challenge of her husband, Mrs. Wertheim pulled back her hand, but looked at him pleadingly as he stood in the doorway.

"Henry, Jacob is dead!"

The old man looked as though someone had hit him. He almost took a step backwards, then leaned on the wall and slowly shook his head.

"He died of a brain tumor a month ago," Hannah continued through tears. "And you wouldn't let me open his letters!"

Slowly, Henry Wertheim crossed the room, sat down beside his wife, and took her hand. "Hannah," he said quietly, "you must pull yourself together."

He turned to Ross. "I'm sure this must be very difficult for you to understand, Mr. Kincaid," he began, "but to us, Jacob died ten years ago, when he turned his back on our faith and became a Christian." (This was the first time Ross had ever heard the word "Christian" pronounced with such obvious revulsion.)

"For generations, our ancestors were persecuted, slandered, tortured, and killed by the Christians of Europe. My grandfather's family left Poland with nothing but the clothes on their backs – driven from their home and country simply because they were Jews. A generation later, they had built up a prosperous jewelry business in Munich – only to find they were not welcome there either, because a man named Hitler decided that Germany would be a better place with no Jews in it at all. And do you know where he got his ideas? From Martin Luther, the Protestant Christian!"

Henry's voice became hoarse, and he seemed to hold his wife's hand more tightly as he continued.

"My parents, my two brothers, my wife's mother, her first husband, and her two small children – what crime had they committed? The most horrible of crimes: they were born Jews, and they held to the faith of their fathers. For this, they met their end in the ovens of Auschwitz and Treblinka – fires that were started generations ago by followers of *that book.*"

Ross had no idea how to respond. He had heard of the Holocaust, of course; his father had fought with Patton in Europe. But he had never realized that the Jews held Christians responsible for the carnage. No wonder Henry Wertheim couldn't forgive his son.

"For what it's worth," Ross said hesitantly, "I'm really sorry about what happened to your families, and to Jacob. Like I said, I only knew him a short while, but he seemed to me like a really decent guy. I know that being a Christian didn't make him ashamed of being a Jew, or hate the Jewish people. But I'm no expert on religion, and maybe he was wrong to leave the one he was born into.

"I can tell you one thing, though: your son loved you both, as sure as I'm sitting here. His last request was for me to bring you his Bible, and this letter. I guess he must have found something pretty important in this book, if it made him willing to give up his career and his family. If I were you, I'd sure want to know what it was."

Henry Wertheim sat and thought in silence for a few moments. Then he reached out and took the letter, and handed it to his wife, who immediately clutched it like her last possession.

"Thank you for bringing us these things," Henry said quietly, "and please accept my apologies for my rudeness, earlier. Our family and our faith are not your concern; you were only trying to keep a promise to a dying man. But I would consider it a favor if you would find some other, more suitable home for that book. If you wish, you are welcome to keep it yourself. I simply cannot allow it in my house."

"Well," Ross sighed, "that's your call, of course." He put the Bible back into his briefcase, but noticed Hannah following it longingly with her eyes.

"I need to be getting back on the road, but I'll leave you folks my business card, just in case you want to reach me for any reason."

"I'll see you to the door," Hannah offered quietly. She left her husband sitting with his head in his hands, looking as though this final blow had broken him for good.

"Mr. Kincaid," Hannah said when they were out on the porch, "I hope you don't think my husband is a bad man. We loved our son dearly, and raised him the best we knew how. At one time, we even hoped he might become a rabbi...." Her voice trailed off in memories. Ross was anxious to be gone now that his obligation was fulfilled, but he couldn't just leave, so he waited in silence. Finally, she turned back to him with a searching look.

"Do you have a family, Mr. Kincaid?"

The question caught Ross completely by surprise. Aware that a simple "yes" or "no" was expected, he couldn't seem to settle on either. "Ah, well... yes...

sort of," he stammered. "But... I haven't seen them for a long time."

"Take some advice from an old woman," Hannah said earnestly. "Find them, and make things right between you."

A tear fell on the envelope she still held in her hand, smudging the ink as she wiped it away. It was then that Ross noticed for the first time – there was no return address.

"Find them," she whispered again. "Don't wait until all you have left is a letter like this one."

12

Chosen

If the premiere of *The Kincaid Miracle* had
produced mixed reviews at Alta Vista High, one place
where it got five stars was Susanna's third period
history class. Many of the students came from poorer
families and broken homes themselves, and
sympathized with Susanna's plight as a single mom
trying to cope. It was as though the incredible
transformation that had taken place in her life had
brought a ray of hope into what had been a rather
dismal classroom.

The only dissenting vote came from a smart,
pretty, popular girl named Angela Locke. Her mother
was the principal of an elementary school, and her
father was a prominent doctor, and a deacon in the
Presbyterian Church. Angela's barely-concealed
contempt for Susanna, both social and intellectual,
didn't change with her teacher's sudden turnaround.
Instead, she threw in her lot with the group that
explained it all away as a desperate act on Susanna's
part to save her job. "I feel sorry for her," Kelly had
heard her airily remark in the cafeteria one day. "But
at least she quit wearing those dreadful rubber bands!"

The tittering of Angela and her friends had made
Kelly flush with embarrassment and anger. However,
she wisely refrained from confronting them, and got

some perspective from her mother later on, as they fixed dinner together in the kitchen.

"I'm glad she's noticed the change!" Susanna laughed. "You remember Pastor Grayson's message last Sunday, about letting our light shine? I guess a hairdo counts, if that's all people will acknowledge."

"Well, I still don't like to hear her talk about you that way," Kelly grumbled. "But," she added, before Susanna could say it for her, "I know we should pray for her, and I will. Really. I just hope you don't have to like somebody for it to count as loving them, because I don't think I could *like* her no matter how hard I tried."

"Well, I know how you feel," Susanna replied. "But remember, Jesus died for us while we were sinners, and there wasn't anything for Him to like about us. And He died for Angela, too, whether she realizes her need for Him right now or not."

As often proved to be the case, it was mostly Susanna herself who had occasion in the coming weeks to need her own advice. Angela was a very clever girl – far too clever to openly disrespect a teacher. But Susanna had always been good at reading people, and with her mind clear of the numbness brought on by alcohol and drugs, she could read this pretty little smart-aleck loud and clear. With Susanna's penchant for emotional outbursts, it was a daily struggle to resist "reacting," and keep on acting in love, instead.

But before too long, another problem developed with Angela that Susanna simply couldn't ignore. By way of motivating the class, Susanna had devised a competition for the best historical essay, separating her students for the purpose into groups of three each. Shortly after the competition began, however, Susanna noticed something very strange going on between Angela and a boy named Tommy Wang, who was on a different team.

Tommy was a really sweet kid, and incredibly smart – one of only a handful of straight-A students in Susanna's class. But, in addition to his being Chinese, he had a severe speech impediment, which factors combined to put him about as low in the social pecking order as a young man could get. Ever since her own rebirth, Susanna had made a special effort to reach out to him, and for a while she really seemed to be getting through.

One of Tommy's problems, however, was that he had a permanent crush on Angela. Needless to say, his feelings were not reciprocated in the least; as far as she was concerned, he might as well not have even existed. That is, until the competition.

To keep everything as fair as possible, Susanna had placed only one of her more gifted students in each threesome. For lack of much intellectual capital to draw from in the third period, Angela ended up with a couple of partners who were somewhat less than brilliant. Susanna had hoped that it would be a lesson in teamwork, but Angela merely resented being separated from her friends for the assignment, and clearly saw herself as being stuck with all the work.

Susanna didn't expect much to come of this latest pout on Angela's part, until she noticed her one day in the cafeteria – sitting next to Tommy Wang. Then there were the furtive smiles exchanged between them in class, and reports from Kelly that Angela was acting like Tommy was her new boyfriend. Tommy, of course, was on cloud nine, but everyone else seemed to think that Angela had lost her mind.

"Except two of her girlfriends," Kelly had qualified. "They're acting kind of smug about the whole thing, like they know something everyone else doesn't."

Susanna had some very sickening suspicions, but tried not to pay attention to them – it was hard enough to put up with the things she *knew* Angela was doing. Then one afternoon, she happened across Tommy in the library, sitting with a stack of medieval history books on the table next to him.

"Why Tommy," she inquired, "I thought you'd be studying up for your competition essay. Aren't you guys working on the causes of World War I?"

Flushing crimson, Tommy stammered something about the Middle Ages being a hobby, but he hastened to replace the books on the shelf, as though he had been caught in the act of a felony. Susanna knew then that she had to do something. The only medieval event she had assigned as a topic was the life of Henry V of England – and it belonged to Angela's group.

Susanna thought about taking up the matter with Tommy, but felt certain he would never believe that Angela was just using him. He would find out sooner or later, of course, but she didn't want to see him hurt any more than he already would be. After much prayer, she made up her mind that the only course was to deal with Angela directly.

Alone with the infinitely superior seventeen-year-old after class, Susanna began to doubt that her plan would be as good in practice as in theory. But, reminding herself that she had no choice but to try, she forged ahead.

"Angela," she began as gently as she could, "do you know that Tommy Wang thinks that you and he are going steady?"

Angela's face twitched into the expression she often wore in Susanna's presence, which was almost a smirk, but not quite. "Well, Mrs. Kincaid," she replied (emphasizing the "Mrs." just a little more than necessary), "I really appreciate your concern about my relationship choices. But I do wonder, respectfully of course, what that has to do with history class?"

"Let's not play games, Angela," Susanna said plainly. "You and I both know that you're only paying attention to Tommy so he'll help you out with the essay competition. He'd rather have one smile from you than all the prizes in the whole school.

"In the first place, I can't allow a student from one team to help another on the sly – it's not fair. In the second place, I can't stand to see Tommy hurt the way you're going to hurt him."

Angela, who was beginning to turn pale, opened her mouth at this point, but Susanna cut her off. "And in the third place, Angela, I know you consider yourself a Christian. How can you do this to Tommy? You may think it's just a game, a joke, and he'll forget about it in no time – but he won't. Believe me, I hurt boys like that when I was your age, and I'll carry the regret of those choices for the rest of my life."

This was the first time Susanna had ever seen Angela lose her cool, superior facade. Her lip was quivering, and she looked as though she could easily contemplate murder. Subduing her emotions with obvious effort, she managed an icy response.

"I *do not* cheat. As for Tommy, I was just being nice – if he got the wrong idea, it's not my fault. Is that all?"

Realizing what she had just set in motion, Susanna switched to a different tone. "I know how you feel about me," she said, "but please do not take it out on Tommy. If you have any compassion for him at all, you'll let him down as gently as you can."

"Sure," was Angela's only reply, and without waiting for any dismissal, she got up and walked angrily out of the classroom.

The next day, Tommy was absent. His mother called in to say that he was sick, but confided to Susanna that she didn't really know what was wrong, and that he wouldn't tell her.

"I wish you would talk to him, Mrs. Kincaid," she said. "I know he likes you, and maybe he'll listen."

At the Wangs' house later that afternoon, Tommy's mother gratefully directed Susanna to the darkened den, where her son lay face-down on the sofa, not even pretending to look at the muted TV.

"Tommy," Susanna called gently, laying her hand on his shoulder. He turned his face up just enough to see who was there, then hid it again in the couch pillows. "I wish I were dead," he declared in a muffled voice.

"Don't wish that, Tommy," Susanna advised. "I wished it myself, once, and came closer than you might imagine to making it come true. Life is a precious gift from God, a chance for us to get to know Him, and decide where we want to spend eternity."

"I don't care!" Tommy exclaimed angrily, suddenly sitting up. "I hate my life, I hate the world, and most of all I hate...." He stopped, but Susanna knew the name he was about to say.

"Hating doesn't change anything, Tommy. Yes, people are cruel, life is unfair, and sometimes it looks like others have all the good things. But it only looks that way to us, because we don't see inside. God knows that every one of us is broken and ruined and lost – even the ones who look like they have it together. Especially them, really, because they're less likely to realize their need before it's too late.

"But you and I, Tommy, we know we need Him. We need Him because no one else loves us, because the ones we thought cared, just tossed us into the trash can on their way out the door."

"Yeah, well maybe that's where I belong," the boy said bitterly, and buried his face in the sofa again.

"I can tell you that it *is* where I belong, Tommy. In fact, it's where we all belong. But that didn't matter to Jesus. He came down from his pure, white, beautiful home in Heaven, and He dug right into the garbage heap, until He found the worst, ugliest, most broken people. And then do you know what He did?"

Without looking up, Tommy shook his head.

"He chose us," Susanna said tearfully. "He picked the ones everyone else threw away. He let Himself be killed for us on that garbage heap. But because He died for us, and then rose again, we get a place in God's family – right up there in the trophy case, shining like the stars, forever. All because He loved us."

The boy was silent for a long while. "I have a hard time believing that," he finally said.

"Well, I'm the living proof," Susanna smiled. "And I brought something else that I thought might help you."

Reaching into her bag, Susanna took out a small book. "This is from the Bible," she explained. "It's called the Gospel of John. I know you love history, and it really happened, so read it like history. Some parts are so beautiful, you can read it like poetry. But most of all, Tommy, read it like a love letter, because it's that, more than anything."

Laying the book on the end table beside him, Susanna quietly left. Once she was gone, Tommy propped himself up on one elbow, and opened the book. On the flyleaf was an inscription.

"To Tommy Wang, from Jesus Christ – I LOVE YOU."

13

Alone

The seaside was one place Ross had always felt at home when he was younger. He loved the way the moon put silvery caps on the waves at night, and the steady, comforting sound of the breakers rolling in. Susanna had loved it too – so much that she readily agreed when he suggested they get married on the beach. They had said their vows to one another just as the sun disappeared below the distant rim of the Pacific. In a symbolic ceremony, they each poured a different color of sand into one large glass jar, so that the grains mixed, never again to be separated.

I wonder what ever happened to that jar, Ross thought to himself as he sat alone on his hotel room balcony. *Susanna probably still has it – she always was sentimental about things like that.*

The three days he had spent in Malibu so far had served only to remind him why he had avoided the place for the last ten years: the memories were too painful. Hannah Wertheim's parting words were stuck in his head like a broken record. *Find your family, and make things right.* That, as the old song said, was easier said than done.

Ever since the day Ross had pried Kelly's little arms from his waist and walked out the front door of his house, he had refused to let himself think about his children. He had given them a house and two cars that were mostly paid for; that was more than most fathers could say. Anyway, it was better for them to have just their mother, and make the best of it, than to be shuttled back and forth between two houses, and fought over by two ever-quarreling parents.

The trouble with excuses like these was that they no longer sounded convincing, even to Ross. The pain in the eyes of Jacob's parents had reminded him of how it felt when he lost his own father, and later his mother. What if Chuck and Kelly felt the same way? What if they never did get over it? Even if the divorce was partly Susanna's fault, it certainly wasn't theirs.

Ross smiled sadly as he remembered Kelly's sixth birthday: the last occasion he had celebrated with his family. She loved the four-foot stuffed panda he bought her so much that she insisted on sleeping with it that night, and nearly fell out of bed trying. *Hard to believe she's already a junior in high school. I bet she has a string of boyfriends a mile long.*

Chuck, of course, would be a grown man by now. Maybe he was almost ready to graduate and go on to medical school, like he once told Ross he wanted to do. But, college takes money, and that was one thing they probably didn't have. Susanna would have gone back to work, of course – it probably did her good to quit moping about the house. They'd be comfortable enough, but certainly not rich.

Over the years, Ross had thought quite a few times about sending money. But each time, his pride stopped him. Mentally, he had closed that account; to open it again would be like admitting that he had owed them something all along. Or worse, perhaps, that he needed something from them. Especially since the accident, and the scars, he couldn't face that. Better to leave that chapter of his life dead and buried, like Colleen, and the burned, twisted carcass of his airplane.

But if that's the way I feel, why am I poking around in the cemetery with a shovel? Realizing that his cigarette was almost gone, and the pack empty, Ross reached into his briefcase for another. Instead, his hand touched the worn leather cover of Jacob's Bible. He pulled it out and absently flipped through the first few pages. The moonlight fell on a phrase that caught his eye: *It is not good that the man should be alone.*

Alone. Until Jacob came and went, he had been okay with being alone – learned to live with it, at least. Now, he was beginning to feel that there was something terribly important missing, and that he ought to try and do something about it.

But what? Just walk back into their lives and say "Daddy's home!"? I'm sure they all hate me. Don't suppose I'd blame the kids much if they did. Why, they wouldn't even recognize me with this made-over face of mine....

A thought struck Ross at that moment, along with the feeling he sometimes had after studying construction problems for hours, when he suddenly hit on the solution. He got up and went into his hotel room, and pulled from his wallet the picture of himself and Colleen that he always carried. Holding it up next to his face, he studied them both in the mirror.

No one would recognize me – not even Susanna....

When it came to business, Ross rarely made snap judgments. But on this, he was suddenly so sure that he didn't have to think about it another moment. Picking up the phone, he quickly reached his partner in Fort Worth. Calling Al Rainey in the evening was never a problem; the man rarely slept and, like Ross, seemed to thrive on work.

"Getting sick of your vacation already, are you?" Al surmised when he answered the phone.

"Well, actually, no," Ross replied. "In fact, I just called to let you know I'm going to be gone for a few weeks longer than we planned. My doctor says I really need the extra rest."

"Since when did you ever listen to that old quack Tobias?" Al snorted. "He wants you to quit smoking, too, remember?"

"Yeah, I know." Ross took a drag on his cigarette, let it out, and watched the smoke float slowly away. "A lot of things might be about to change. A lot of things."

14

Courage

Lawrence J. Feinberg was a born troublemaker. Susanna knew it, as did most of his fellow students, and every teacher who had been unfortunate enough to have him occupy a desk in their classroom. Larry himself knew it, and seemed to genuinely relish the role.

The problem with Larry wasn't that he was stupid; he was a talented artist, and if he'd chosen to apply himself, he could have been a straight-A student, too. Unfortunately for the faculty of Alta Vista High, he didn't choose to apply himself to anything but making their lives miserable, a goal he achieved with amazing success, year after year.

How Larry came to be a part of Susanna's class was a story in itself. Until just a few weeks ago, his history teacher had been Susanna's unflappable colleague, Ferrell Johnson. Principal Tyler apparently thought the hobby archaeologist's legendary patience could withstand the ultimate test. This seven-month experiment concluded with a very unhappy week for Mr. Johnson, in which he sent Larry to the principal's office no less than five times. On the last occasion, the parting shot roared out by the tormented teacher was heard by the entire floor: "And don't come back!"

And so Mr. Tyler (a former chemistry professor who liked to tinker) decided on yet another

experiment. Since there had been such a remarkable
change in Susanna Kincaid, why not let her take a shot
at redeeming another "lost cause"? When he informed
Susanna of his decision, she opened her mouth to
protest, but to her amazement, heard herself say,
"Why, that will be fine, Mr. Tyler. I'll do my best to
help him however I can."

And she did do her best. The trouble was, Larry
didn't want to be helped, and actively resisted her
every effort to rouse him from his defiant boredom.
Since her new birth, Susanna's classroom had been
changed from one of the dullest in the school (heavy
on movies and reading periods) to one of the most
interesting. Having come alive in the Lord, she had
rediscovered her love of history, and was finding new
and creative ways to share that love with her students.

Among her innovations was a special time every
Friday when one or two students were allowed to give
presentations in the voice of their favorite character
from history. If they wished, they might even bring
appropriate props, or costume elements. Needless to
say, Larry declined to participate, preferring to jeer the
performances of his fellow students.

The Friday before spring break, the student
giving the presentation was Ashley Franklin, a sweet,
shy girl who happened to be completely blind. Her
character was Lady Jane Grey, the hapless, short-lived
monarch who was executed on the orders of her
cousin, Queen Mary, in 1554. Ashley started off very
nervously, but began getting into character as she
reenacted the last few, courageous moments of Lady

Jane's life, in which she recited a Psalm from the scaffold, and forgave her executioner.

Larry was, not surprisingly, quite unmoved by the heartfelt performance of the blind girl. Taking advantage of the fact that Susanna was seated at a desk, with her back to him, he began a ridiculous pantomime of Ashley's gestures. This, naturally, distracted the class, and caused a ripple of mirth, where there should have been solemn attention. By the time Susanna realized what was going on, the poor, sensitive girl had given up and sat down in tears.

Now, the old Susanna would have done one of two things: bawled Larry out in front of the class and sent him to the principal's office, or burst out crying herself. But the new Susanna did neither. She just sat, silently, and prayed. When all the laughter had died down, and the only sound left was Ashley's sniffling, Susanna got up and wrote a word on the board in large, capital letters. Then she turned, and faced her students.

"Class," she began quietly, "let's talk for a minute about *courage*."

A couple of the kids who had been laughing before shifted uncomfortably in their seats. Larry just slouched at his desk, his permanent smirk still intact.

"Lady Jane Grey was just about your age when she was executed," Susanna continued. "Yet she faced death calmly, bravely, and with forgiveness in her heart. Where do you think she got the courage to do that?"

She waited, but no hands went up.

"You all know Ashley is blind, and she's also very shy. It was hard for her to stand up in front of you all today, but she did it anyway. Where do you think her courage came from?"

Again, there was no answer. Larry, upset at no longer being the center of attention, began drumming his fingers on his desk.

"Yes, Larry?"

He looked up, startled. "Who, me? I didn't raise my hand."

"I believe you raised your hand earlier. In fact, I seem to recall your raising both hands and waving quite enthusiastically." A muffled snicker went through the class.

"But, since you don't seem to have the answer for that question, let's try another. Do you think *you* have courage?"

"Well, sure," Larry snorted. "Everybody knows I'm not scared of anything."

"Is that so?" Susanna raised an eyebrow. "Well, that's a pretty bold claim. Would you like to prove it to us?"

Sensing a trap, Larry hesitated. "You mean like, right now? What do you want me to do – go climb the flagpole? I did that last year, remember?"

"Yes, I remember. But what I have in mind takes a lot more guts than that. I'd like you to show us that you're brave enough to stand up and apologize to someone you just hurt very deeply."

Larry realized he was cornered. He thought a moment, and started to get up, but Susanna stopped him when she saw his smirk coming back.

"Before you make a joke out of it, Larry, let me warn you that that's the coward's way out, and we all know it. If you don't have what it takes to really apologize, I suggest you just stay in your seat."

Larry paused midair, and slowly sat back down, his face flushed with anger. Susanna turned back to her desk, but heard his voice behind her, dripping with sarcasm.

"I guess I just don't know much about courage, Mrs. Kincaid. Maybe you could help me out? I hear some people get theirs out of little orange bottles from the pharmacy."

There was an audible, collective gasp in the classroom. Susanna turned around slowly, and saw Larry's look of anticipation. He was absolutely sure she was going to blow up, and as her face slowly spread into a smile, his fell in disbelief.

"It sounds like you've been peeking at my autobiography, Larry."

The boy looked utterly confused. "Are you actually... admitting that...?"

"That I was hooked on pills? Yes, I was. Pills to sleep, pills to stay awake, pills to forget, pills to remember. When those didn't dull the pain enough, I tried to drown my sorrows in alcohol. That didn't work either. I got so desperate that I was almost ready to take the final escape."

"So what changed?" Matt Kemp asked the question without raising his hand, but Susanna didn't mind a bit. He was a burly football player who had spent most of his life in foster homes and juvenile detention. He had been watching her carefully for weeks, and finally saw his chance to find out the secret – and this was one secret that Susanna couldn't have been happier to share.

"What happened is that I met someone, Matt: a man called Jesus Christ. I never cared about Him, and I certainly never thought He cared about me. But when I got to the end of my rope, I cried out to Him, and He saved me – not only from the guilt and bitterness that were the consequences of my sin, but from the sin itself.

"With Jesus living in my heart, I just don't need the pills or the alcohol any more. Sure, life still hurts sometimes. But He gives me a peace and a joy that make it worthwhile to live. And not only that, but I know now where I'll spend eternity, in a place where there are no hurts, ever again."

The class was totally quiet. Even Larry had nothing to say – he just sat and stared as though his teacher had just landed from Mars. In fact, the only one in the room not staring was Angela, who appeared to be taking notes, and was wearing a disturbingly smug expression. Just at that moment the bell rang, and the students slowly filed out, with uncharacteristic sobriety.

When Susanna got back from lunch, she was surprised to find some unsigned artwork on her whiteboard. On one side of the word "COURAGE" was the unmistakable likeness of Ashley Franklin, and on the other side was her own.

"Well, that's a start, Larry," Susanna whispered to herself. *With God, nothing shall be impossible.*

15
Overhaul

"I think that's got it," Chuck called out as he scooted his creeper out from under the panel truck. "Try it again, Mr. Heywood."

The old farmer turned the key in the ignition, and smiled as the engine roared happily to life. "You're a magician, Chuck," he yelled. "You're gonna have your own shop one day!"

As always, his mostly-deaf customer was louder than necessary, but when he was saying things like that, the young mechanic didn't mind. He only hoped his boss, Rocky Philips, was listening. *More likely he's already left for the golf course,* Chuck thought bitterly. *I keep him in business, so he can spend time working on his chip shot.*

Of course, Chuck had to admit that when he first landed this job, he'd been plenty glad to get it. Not many shops would hire a mechanic who didn't even have a full set of tools to call his own. But Chuck had his father's nature, all right, whether he admitted it or not. He was restless and ambitious, and after two years of lining Rocky's pockets, he was ready to move on.

"Hey Dave," Chuck hollered, "you about done with that transmission job?" His fellow slave, David Nazarian, emerged from the underside of his current project with a sooty grin.

"What this old heap needs is *transmission* to the junkyard! I wonder if it ever occurred to Mrs. Hampstead that she could put a down payment on a brand new Lincoln Continental for what she's paying us to resuscitate this one."

"But, young man," Chuck mimicked, "they just don't make them like this anymore!"

"Well, she's right about that," David laughed. "I don't think Ford would be in business much longer if they did. It'll probably take me the rest of the day just to find all the problems."

"Let's grab lunch, then. My next customer won't be here for an hour."

"You know Rocky doesn't like us to close up the shop for lunch," David said doubtfully.

"Who cares?" Chuck glanced over his shoulder to confirm that the office light was out. "He's not here."

"I think you know the answer to that," David smiled.

Chuck rolled his eyes. "Oh, I forgot, you've got that goody-two-shoes thing going on. You remind me of my mom and little sister. One day it was booze, pot, and wild parties, and the next it's religion. Everything is 'Jesus this' and 'Jesus that.' I can't seem to convince them that I'm not interested."

"Maybe that's because they care about you," David suggested.

"Yeah, sure, I know they do. And I'm not knocking it; I haven't seen Mom this happy in years. And Kelly's grades are so much better, I'd swear she was cheating if she hadn't owned up to it when she didn't have to."

"Your sister confessed to cheating in school?" David marveled.

"Yeah, isn't that the craziest thing you ever heard? Not that I approve of her cheating, mind you, but she was in the clear! And at the time, she needed that grade really bad. I think this Jesus thing has gone to her head."

"Or maybe her heart," David countered.

Chuck groaned. "Why am I standing here, wasting my lunch hour ranting about one religious fanatic to another?"

"Actually, you haven't clocked out yet," David pointed out.

"Oh my, you're right, Reverend," admitted Chuck with mock solemnity. "I shall repent forthwith, and work an extra five minutes off the clock this evening, to atone for my manifest sins and wickedness."

David ignored the jibe. "I'd like to meet your family sometime," he said. "Where do they go to church?"

Chuck laughed out loud. "Oh, that's the best part. They go to an auto parts store!"

"That's real funny, Chuck."

"No joke, man, their church meets at Flanahan's Auto Parts! The old guy is closed on Sundays now, and he lets them use the empty part of his warehouse for their church service. The pastor is some guy named Farmer who used to sell light bulbs, and his right-hand deacon is a bricklayer named Pillow. Believe me, you can't make this stuff up!"

"Sounds interesting," David mused. "I may have to check it out."

"Hey, be my guest. Just don't blame me if you wind up getting baptized in a parts washer!" Still laughing, Chuck turned and walked over toward a rough-looking pickup that had just pulled into the empty bay. The driver, a middle-aged, well-built man with a scarred face, gave him a quizzical look as he climbed out.

"I didn't know this truck was so funny. Maybe I should take it on tour?"

"No, sir," Chuck said, sobering up. "It was just an inside joke with my buddy. What can we do for you?"

"Well, I just bought this pickup a few days ago – got a really good deal on it. It has quite a few problems, I'm told, but nothing that a good mechanic can't fix. You were highly recommended by a friend of mine, so I'd like you to take a look at it and give me your opinion."

So people are starting to talk about me, Chuck thought with satisfaction. *Rocky Philips, get ready to find yourself another grease-monkey.* He gave the truck a thorough inspection, and then took it for a drive around the block.

"I'm afraid it needs a complete engine overhaul," he reported to the owner. "We can handle it, but you're talking some serious money."

The stranger shrugged. "That's okay. Like I said, I gave next to nothing for it. How about I leave it with you, and you can work up a formal estimate. I'll be back, say, tomorrow afternoon?"

"Yes sir, that would be fine. What name shall I put down on the paperwork?"

"Morton," the man replied. "Roger Morton."

Late that afternoon, David found Chuck sitting at the service desk, chewing on a pen, a mostly-blank estimate form still in front of him. "Hey, dreamer, it's quitting time! Or are you still atoning?"

Chuck looked up absently at his friend. "You know, Dave," he said, "there's something about that guy Morton that really bugs me. He looked at me like he knew me, but I've never seen the man before in my life, I'm sure."

"Well, maybe you look like someone he used to know. They say everyone has a twin."

"Yeah," Chuck agreed as he punched out. "It's probably something like that. It's a cinch he doesn't travel in my social circle. A 'formal estimate'? What makes a guy who talks like that go out and buy a junker like this?"

"Who knows?" David shrugged. "People do strange things sometimes."

"Speaking of which," Chuck said with a glance at his watch, "I'd better get home to the strange women in my house and grab an early supper. They're having a Bible study there tonight." He reached for the light switch, but noticed that David was staring at him.

Chuck sighed. "Okay, you're invited. But if I catch you talking to my mother and sister about me, I'm going to drop a school bus on you."

David grinned happily. "Don't worry, I'll let them do the talking. But God's got your number anyway, Chuck."

"Well, just so he doesn't call me – I'll call him if I need him."

Chuck switched off the lights, and locked the door behind him.

16

Stealing Home

Throughout the long taxicab ride back to his hotel, Ross relived the brief meeting with Chuck, still finding it hard to believe that his ruse had actually worked. He had stood within arm's reach of his son, held a conversation, and hadn't caught even a glimmer of recognition. Ross was glad he had learned years ago how to keep a poker face, a skill that had turned out to be useful in more than business.

As for Chuck, Ross would have known him anywhere, even without the mechanic's name tag. It was like looking in a mirror from thirty years ago. *If he's half the man I think he is, he won't be long for a dinky little garage like that. Maybe he could use a little anonymous help....*

Ever since he had resolved to find his family, Ross had been rediscovering what it felt like to be alive. He had a purpose now, a plan, a hope. But paradoxically, he also found himself feeling a greater weight of loneliness than ever before. Now that he finally had something in his life worth sharing, there was no one to share it with.

"Any messages for me?" he inquired at the hotel desk. The frazzled-looking clerk rummaged through a pile of paper scraps that apparently constituted her filing system.

"Ah, yes, Mr. Morton," she announced as she found the right sticky note. "A gentleman who gave his name as 'Phil' called, and asked you to meet him at the usual place at seven o'clock."

"Okay, thanks." Ross grabbed the note and stuffed it in his pocket, shaking his head at the cloak-and-dagger antics of his private investigator. The guy actually seemed to think he was the incarnation of Sam Spade. Still, Ross couldn't argue with the results. It had taken Phil less than a week to set him up with a fake identity, and to come up with a workable plan for reconnecting with Chuck as Roger Morton. Ross guessed he had more findings to report, and was probably anxious to collect his fee, which he insisted be paid daily, in cash.

The "usual place" was a smoky, out-of-the-way diner called Clancy's Cafe. The place looked like a dump, and the food was awful, but Ross never felt much like eating at their meetings anyway. Phil, on the other hand, seemed to be addicted to Clancy's chili, which he laced with hot sauce and devoured by the quart, without regard to its questionable content. He had already finished his meal (if one could call it that) by the time Ross arrived this evening, and was nursing a beer in the dive's darkest corner, seated with his back to the wall.

"So what have you got for me today, Phil?" Ross inquired, taking a seat on the cracked vinyl bench.

"Shh... not so loud!" The detective's eyes swept nervously around the nearly-empty restaurant. "Did you bring my fee?"

"Yes," Ross sighed, handing him a folded copy of the *Los Angeles Times,* which had the requisite greenbacks tucked inside. "I still think you've been watching too many TV cop shows."

"Look, Mr. K., do I tell you how to build skyscrapers? Anyway, my stuff's been good so far, right?"

"I'll give you that," Ross admitted. "Did you find out anything about Kelly?"

Phil adjusted his frayed fedora and looked uncomfortable. "Yeah, but I'm afraid you're not going to like it much."

Ross felt his heart rate rise, and immediately wondered why. For ten years he hadn't much cared what happened to his daughter, but now, suddenly, her welfare seemed pretty important.

"She's been in trouble at school quite a bit," Phil continued. "Minor stuff mostly, like smoking pot and skipping classes. But earlier this year, she got involved with a heroin dealer by the name of Robby Crawford. She was in his parents' car when he wrecked it on a mile-high joyride, and killed another of his girlfriends."

Ross found his throat so dry, he had to clear it in order to speak. "Was Kelly hurt?"

"Amazingly, no. And what's more, she wasn't even charged with possession, even though her boyfriend went up for manslaughter. But I have to warn you, Mr. K., things don't look real good for your daughter from where I sit. If she was running with that Crawford character, odds are she's already hooked on H. And believe me, that's not a pretty sight."

Ross felt himself suddenly getting angry. "Do you have any proof at all that she's addicted to drugs? You just said she wasn't charged!"

Phil threw up his hands. "Hey, Mr. K., take it easy. I'm just trying to prepare you for the worst. For all I know, she may have traded in her bong for a hymnbook by now. If it turns out that way, there won't be anyone happier than me that I was wrong."

Ross turned away from the scruffy private eye, as a sudden flashback put him in the living room of his old house. Kelly, her little arms wrapped around his waist, begged him not to leave her. He shook his head, as though he could clear the memory from his mind.

"Anything wrong?" Phil asked. "Would you like a drink, maybe?"

"I don't drink," Ross sighed, though at the moment he was feeling unusually tempted. He decided to change the subject instead. "What about Susanna?"

"News isn't a whole lot better there, I'm afraid. Up until a few months ago, she was a 'patient' of a pill peddler by the name of Dr. Strait, who was actually so crooked he wound up in San Quentin. He was giving her 'prescriptions' for all sorts of stuff: uppers, tranquilizers, you name it. On top of that, she was a regular customer at a singles bar just around the corner from here. It's got some class compared to this place, for sure, but they tell me she was stiff enough to need a taxi most nights by closing time."

Susanna? An alcoholic, and a drug addict? Ross didn't want to believe it, but he should have known. He could see her in his mind's eye, too, sobbing at the kitchen table, a helpless emotional wreck whose one solid support had just abandoned her. For the first time, the curtains were being pulled back on the play he had set in motion that day. It had turned out to be a horror show, and Ross was beginning to wish he hadn't bought a ticket.

"Hey, Mr. K, are you listening?"

"Yeah, Phil," Ross replied absently. "But I don't know – maybe I shouldn't have...."

"I was just going to say," Phil interrupted, "that there might be some light at the end of the tunnel for your ex-wife. Some of the other regulars at the bar told me they haven't seen her around in quite a while. They think maybe she got hooked up with AA or something. One of them said he ran into her at the mall, and she seemed really different."

"Different?" Ross felt some of his hope coming back. "How different?"

Phil scratched his head. "Well, he wasn't real specific on that, and he was a little drunk, so I'm not sure how good his information is."

"Well, thanks again, Phil," Ross said as he got up. "I think I can take it from here."

Phil grinned slyly. "So the new face fooled your son, eh?"

"Yeah, he doesn't suspect a thing. I don't know about Susanna, but there's only one way to find out for sure."

"Just try and take it slow," Phil cautioned. "If you come on too strong, you'll blow your cover for sure. I'll be on call if you need me." Stuffing the cash-laden newspaper into his grimy jacket, the detective slipped quietly out the back exit.

Ross actually didn't have anything like a well-formed plan to introduce his new persona to Susanna and Kelly. But after what he had heard tonight, he had to at least drive by the house, and maybe get some idea of what was going on there.

Even in the dark, Ross had no problem finding his way back to the home he and Susanna had shared for almost thirteen years. There was a persistent sense of unreality to it; nothing seemed to have changed. It was like he had put in an extra-long day at the office – a ten-year day – and now he was headed home.

Except that it's not home anymore, Ross thought bitterly. *Susanna's an alcoholic, Kelly's a juvenile delinquent, and Chuck probably hates the sound of my name. Is this the reason I lived through that plane crash? So I could come back and see the wreck I left behind at home?*

As Ross made the final turn onto his old street, he cut off the engine, and rolled down the windows to catch any sound that might come from the house as he coasted by. But the sound he heard was the last one he expected: singing. Ross couldn't make out the words, but it was definitely a group of people, and not a radio or a recording. All around the house there were cars parked, in the yard and in the street – at least eight or ten.

*An AA meeting? Surely they don't sing like that.
Some sort of church meeting? Now there's a crazy
thought. Susanna might be an alcoholic and a drug
addict, but religious? Never.*

Turning the corner to circle the block once more,
Ross reached for his car phone.

"Phil? Yeah, it's Ross Kincaid. I think I may
have some more work for you after all...."

17

Here Is Love

Chuck hated fish. Almost all of Susanna's and Kelly's church friends, however, seemed to love it. This meant that fish was usually on the menu whenever any of that group came over, which just gave Chuck another reason to dislike it. On this particular night, however, he had come prepared with a frozen pizza, which he intended to consume in front of the TV in his room, alone.

"Oh, Chuck," Susanna moaned when she caught sight of his prospective dinner, "I forgot to tell you, the microwave oven's on the blink."

"Well, this must be my lucky day," Chuck griped. "Wonder how this pizza would taste *a la Eskimo*?"

"Just awful," Kelly giggled. "What do you have against fish, anyway?"

"What do your church people have against good old-fashioned hamburgers?" he countered. "This isn't Friday."

"It's Catholics that eat fish on Fridays, silly," Kelly teased. "Remember Patti Mullins?"

"Is that the girl who came here for a sleepover and couldn't eat the pot roast? I thought she was a vegetarian, anyway."

"That was only for a few months, when we were in eighth grade. She doesn't seem to know what she believes anymore, so I've been trying to talk to her about the Lord. When I can catch up with her, that is."

"Got her spooked, have you?" asked Chuck, in an "I-told-you-so" tone.

"Well, maybe a little," Kelly admitted. "But you know, people thought Jesus' first disciples were pretty strange too. We just learned the other day that they were accused of turning the world upside down!"

"Sounds about right to me," Chuck muttered. "Oh, that reminds me, I've invited another 'disciple' to your meeting – hope you don't mind. I'm pretty sure he would have tried to sneak in, if I hadn't."

"Of course we don't mind, dear!" Susanna replied, slipping a tray of neatly-arranged flounder fillets in the oven. "Just who is this surprise guest?"

"David Nazarian, from work. You remember, I told you how he brings leftovers of unpronounceable dishes for lunch."

"Oh, yeah," Kelly recalled. "You said he was Artesian, or something."

"Armenian," Chuck corrected. "I made the mistake of mentioning there was a Bible study at my house tonight, and he nearly jumped into my car.'"

"I hope not," Kelly laughed. "One jump into that old VW of yours would probably finish it."

"Hey, quit picking on my car," Chuck protested. "It's good on gas, and I've got more important things to save for. Anyway, David went home to get cleaned up. I told him to come about seven."

"You could have invited him to dinner," Susanna offered. "We have plenty."

"Mom, you're already feeding nineteen people," Chuck groaned. "We're not exactly rich, you know."

"And we're not exactly destitute, either," his mom smiled. "But either way, a few extra fish dinners won't put us on the welfare rolls. Which brings us back to your dinner, I guess. Will it be fish, or frozen pizza?"

"I'll just have a sandwich," Chuck grumbled. "I hope you made something for dessert."

"I did!" Kelly piped up.

"You? In the kitchen?" Chuck's disbelief was plainly written on his face. He sniffed the air facetiously. "Do I smell something burning?"

"Now, Chuck," Susanna reproved mildly, "don't give Kelly such a hard time. She's already learned a lot very quickly. I think she's going to make an excellent cook one day."

"This I gotta see," Chuck snorted. "Just what did you make, Chef Kincaid?"

"German chocolate cake," Kelly replied, rather stormily. "And if you try to say it's burned, I'll...."

"Try to do a better job next time," finished Susanna, with a smile, and a cautionary glance at the crestfallen Kelly.

"Yeah... that's right," she agreed quietly. "But I hope you like it, anyway."

Chuck suddenly felt rather ashamed of himself, and almost irritated that Kelly didn't finish her own sentence the way he knew she wanted to. Time was when she'd have sulked off to her room, or maybe dumped the whole cake in the trash in protest. But now she seemed to have gotten over it already, and was brightly greeting the guests as they arrived. Forget about her high school chums; the new Kelly was spooking *him*.

Still, Chuck wound up spending most of the dinner hour hanging around downstairs. Despite feeling a bit nervous around these people – almost as if he were a stranger in his own home – Chuck couldn't help finding them quite fascinating. Whenever they got together, they would talk about ordinary events like someone finding their eyeglasses, or getting a new screen door, as though they were really exciting. Sometimes such reports would elicit a response like "Praise the Lord!" – a phrase that literally made Chuck cringe. If anyone had told him, even three months ago, that he'd be hearing it in his own house, he'd have said they were crazy.

At seven o'clock on the dot, the Kincaid doorbell announced the arrival of the disgustingly punctual David Nazarian. Chuck made the necessary introductions rather hastily; knowing that both the Bible study and his favorite TV show were about to start, he was intent on missing the former and not the latter.

But on his way out the door, he noticed an unfamiliar face in the group. A very pretty girl, whom he took to be a couple of years older than Kelly, was sitting next to her near the front of the room, tuning up a guitar. Suddenly the Bible study seemed like it might be more interesting than *Junkyard Derby* after all. Pulling a chair across from the dining room, he straddled it backwards, deliberately keeping in the shadows so he could leave unnoticed when the preaching started.

After the opening prayer, Pastor Grayson Farmer (the erstwhile lighting salesman Chuck had derided earlier) stood up with a smile. "I've managed to talk Beth and Kelly into sharing a very special song with us this evening. This hymn is around a hundred years old, and it became famous around the turn of the century as 'The Love Song of the Welsh Revival.' Please listen with your heart as we worship our wonderful Savior."

A love song? Chuck was even more interested. Beth got up along with Kelly, smoothed back her long brown hair, adjusted her guitar, and began to play. The blend of the two girls' voices was beautiful, and so were the words, even if their true meaning was lost on at least one of the listeners.

> *Here is love, vast as the ocean*
> *Lovingkindness, as the flood*
> *When the Prince of Life, our ransom*
> *Shed for us his precious blood.*
> *Who his love will not remember?*
> *Who can cease to sing his praise?*
> *He can never be forgotten*
> *Throughout Heaven's eternal days.*
>
> *On the mount of crucifixion*
> *Fountains opened, deep and wide*
> *Through the floodgates of God's mercy*

Flowed a vast, and gracious tide.
Grace and love, like mighty rivers
Poured incessant from above
Heaven's peace and perfect justice
Kissed a guilty world in love.

The song ended and the girls sat back down. Chuck started to clap, but immediately sensed that was the wrong thing to do. The room was completely silent, but it was as though everyone was still listening, and hearing something he couldn't. Rather than looking around to see who had noticed her, Beth's eyes were closed, her chin resting on her clasped hands, and a look on her face that Chuck could only describe as completely restful.

I wonder what it would be like to have peace like that. The thought flashed into Chuck's mind suddenly, and he wondered where it had come from. It wasn't peace he wanted – it was money, and lots of it. But on the side, why not score a few dates with a pretty girl? He could at least pretend to be interested in religion for a while.

On that theory, Chuck made himself sit through the whole Bible study, moving in a little closer so he could be seen. It was almost all over his head: something about five virgins, and lamps, and being ready for Jesus to come back any day. He tried to memorize at least a couple of phrases to use later on.

David, on the other hand, seemed to be right in his element, as expected. He asked questions, including one that seemed to stump the pastor, who promised to research it and get back to him. Chuck, while watching Beth, couldn't help noticing Kelly watching David, with a look that seemed to be quite admiring.

After the meeting, coffee and dessert were served all around. Chuck got a piece of cake for himself, and one for David, who began eating it rather absently. He was intent on a discussion with Don Pillow, Tina's husband, who was indeed a bricklayer, but also knew the Bible better than most preachers.

"This cake is the greatest, sis!" Chuck lied, calculating that he'd do well to butter up his sister, in hopes of a good introduction to Beth.

"Oh, I'm so glad you like it!" Kelly blushed. "I wasn't sure if walnuts would work for the icing, but I ran out of pecans."

"Walnuts?" David suddenly looked up, startled. "Uh oh... I'm afraid I'm pretty allergic to walnuts." That last statement was quite unnecessary, as anyone could see his lips swelling, and hear the sudden wheeze in his voice. Kelly turned as white as a sheet, and Susanna reached for the phone to call 911.

"No, please," David tried to calm them, "it's not that bad. Do you have any antihistamines?"

Some Benadryl was quickly located, a prayer offered by Pastor Grayson, and everyone settled down. Everyone, that is, except for Kelly, who refused to be convinced that David's allergy attack wasn't her fault, and must have apologized at least twenty times before the evening was over. She insisted on staying with him until the symptoms had completely subsided, and as a result, they spent quite a bit of time getting acquainted.

Finally, about ten o'clock, David became the last guest to make his farewells. "I can't remember when I've enjoyed an evening so much," he said sincerely, "walnuts or no walnuts."

"Me too!" Kelly agreed, with her usual enthusiasm. "That is, I'm sorry about the nuts, but I'm really glad you came. Will we see you again?"

"I'll be visiting your church on Sunday, Lord willing," David replied. "And assuming I don't meet with a strange accident involving a school bus." He grinned in Chuck's direction. "See you at work tomorrow, buddy."

Chuck went to bed that night feeling better than he usually did after a party. He never did get the introduction to Beth he wanted, but that could wait. He probably needed to work on his "seeker" image just a bit first, anyway. This would be an interesting challenge.

18

The Mission Field

Kelly fanned her face with a notebook, wishing for a breeze, and glanced at her watch for the third time in five minutes. Spring had just barely started – it wasn't supposed to be this hot yet. And Beth was supposed to be there to pick her up at 3:15. And prayers were supposed to be answered, especially when you're trying to fulfill the Great Commission, right?

With some relief, she caught sight of Beth's dusty-blue Maverick rounding the corner. Already finishing her first year of community college, Kelly's new friend had offered to pick her up whenever Susanna had to work late. She had even let Kelly drive once or twice, which was a greater risk than Chuck was willing to take with his priceless Bug.

"Sorry I'm late," Beth apologized as her friend climbed in. "My poor old battery is about ready for the scrap heap, I'm afraid. It took me fifteen minutes to find someone to give me a jump."

"You should talk to my brother Chuck," Kelly suggested. "He's a mechanic, so he could probably get you a good deal."

"I think I saw him at the Bible study the other night," Beth remembered, "but we never got introduced. Wasn't he the one who raved about your cake?"

"Yeah," Kelly confirmed, wishing that description wasn't so singularly identifying. "I know it was lousy. He was just trying to make me feel better, because he gave me a hard time about it earlier."

"Well, at least he cares," Beth encouraged. "And believe me, practice does make perfect. The first biscuits I ever made were so hard, my brothers used them for batting practice."

"Well, you were lucky," Kelly countered. "My brother used *me* for batting practice... as the pitcher, I mean, not as the ball. But I never learned one end of a spatula from the other until Mom and I found the Lord. Now I feel like I have everything in the world to catch up on, and...." Her voice trailed off, and Beth picked up the note of discouragement.

"What's the matter? Is it about the mission trip?"

Kelly just sighed. Ever since she had learned about the trip Mr. Pillow was leading to Jamaica, to help a small congregation construct their own church building, she had been dying to go. But money, or rather the lack thereof, was proving to be a very stubborn obstacle.

"I just don't understand it, Beth," she complained. "I've prayed and prayed about this trip, and I was sure the Lord wanted me to go. But I just can't find a job except for babysitting, and that doesn't pay anywhere near enough. At this rate, by the time Mr. Pillow leaves, my 'Jamaica Fund' will have enough in it to get me about as far as Phoenix, Arizona."

Beth stifled a laugh, knowing her friend was in earnest. "What about Billy's Burger?" she suggested. "It's right on your way home."

Kelly shook her head. "Chuck used to work there, but he tried to take the manager's job, and there was a big blowup, and he wound up getting fired. Now we don't even eat there, for fear of being poisoned."

Beth giggled. "Have you ever considered a career in drama?"

"What I want to be is a missionary," Kelly lamented. "I want to hold those cute little kids, and teach them songs about Jesus, and...." Kelly stopped suddenly.

"Uh-oh, there's a police car in front of the Smiths' house. Mom is going to be so upset if DiAngelo is in trouble again."

"Is that the kid your mom was tutoring?"

"Yeah, and he's been doing really well lately. Better pull over, Beth, so we can find out what's happened."

The girls didn't have long to wait, as two uniformed officers soon emerged from the house, with DiAngelo in handcuffs between them.

"Oh no," Kelly moaned. She was out of the car the next second, and headed for the house. Beth, always more cautious and sensible, jumped out of the car too, and momentarily restrained her headstrong friend.

"Officers, we know the people that live here – is it okay if we go in?"

The lead policeman merely nodded as he placed his prisoner in the car.

"What happened?" Kelly asked anxiously. "What did he do? He's only twelve, you know," she added, ignoring a jab from Beth's elbow.

"I can't give you any information on that, ma'am," the officer replied stoically. "If you know the family, I suggest you talk to them."

Inside, Kelly and Beth found DiAngelo's mother, sitting on the couch, and crying uncontrollably. Beth went into the kitchen and made some tea, while Kelly tried her best to calm her neighbor down.

After much coaxing, they managed to get the full story. DiAngelo had been arrested for arson, along with some other boys, after they set fire to an unoccupied, run-down rental house. Since there seemed to be no discernible reason for the crime, the police were laying it to a gang initiation. There had been reports that a gang called "The Jackknives" was moving into the neighborhood, and they were known for requiring prospective members to commit felonies in order to be admitted.

"But my baby, he got nothin' to do with no gang," Mrs. Smith insisted. "I work two jobs so he gets plenty to eat, clothes to wear, and we keep a roof over our heads. What's he need to go and join a gang for?"

Neither of the girls had much of an answer for that question. All they could do was pray with Mrs. Smith, and promise to keep giving whatever help they could to her and her son.

"But how *can* we help?" Kelly asked when they were back in Beth's car. "These gangs just spread like a disease, and there doesn't seem to be any stopping them. Those 'Jackknives' were in my junior high school, but they weren't anywhere near this neighborhood in those days."

"Did they try to get you to join?" Beth asked, almost fearfully.

"Oh, no – it was boys only. We did sort of start our own gang though: we called ourselves 'The She-wolves.' It was stupid, really; all we did was hold 'secret' meetings where we mostly talked about boys. Sometimes one of the girls brought a cigarette and we'd pretend to smoke, but we were all too scared to really inhale."

"I guess every kid just wants to be a part of something," Beth observed.

"Yeah," Kelly agreed. "Especially when your own family is a wreck. I just did what everyone else was doing, from graffiti right up through smoking pot, and almost shooting heroin. What if I hadn't been scared of needles, Beth? What if I'd have died in that car wreck, without ever knowing Jesus?" She shuddered at the thought.

"There's no need to go there, Kelly," Beth consoled. "I've heard it said that there are no 'what if's' in God's world. He knew from the very beginning that He would send someone to share with your mom, and that He'd keep you alive to hear the good news too."

"You know, Kelly," Beth added thoughtfully, "your own mission field may be a lot closer than you think. You want to work with kids – how about the kids in your own neighborhood? Who could reach them better than someone who knows what it's like to be in a gang?"

Kelly shook her head and almost laughed. "Beth, I told you, it wasn't really a gang. But...."

"But what?" Beth smiled. "I can see the wheels in your head turning!"

"Well, even if I wasn't in a real gang, I do sort of speak the lingo, if you know what I mean."

"Right...."

"And I don't see why we can't do what my friends and I did in junior high – start a competing gang! We could build a clubhouse, and make up a secret code, and instead of vandalism, we could help people. Maybe we could even get permission to paint over some of the graffiti on the bridges! I drew some of that myself, so it would be nice to have a hand in getting rid of it."

"Well, let's not get ahead of ourselves," Beth cautioned, though she was already feeling the excitement too. "We'd better talk to your mom first of all, and then maybe to Pastor Grayson. I've heard him talk about the church doing some sort of inner-city outreach. Maybe we could tie into that somehow."

Never one to let grass grow under her feet, Kelly had won approval for her project from both her mother and their pastor within the week. The first obstacle wasn't long in being discovered, however: the cost of building any kind of a clubhouse turned out to be many times the new club's minuscule budget. The problem was laid before the Lord in prayer at the next church meeting, and this time, Kelly *knew* God was going to answer. But the answer came even more quickly than she was expecting.

A building contractor named Clint Agee, who usually attended church elsewhere, happened to be present that evening, having been invited by his friend Don Pillow. Immediately after the prayer service, he introduced himself to the group, and explained that he had been contacted that very day by the owner of the house that DiAngelo and his friends had tried to burn. As it turned out, they had done a very poor job of it, and although the interior was gutted, the structure was still quite sound.

Unfortunately for the owner, however, he had accidentally let the insurance lapse, and when he saw the repair estimate, he told Mr. Agee that he didn't want to invest that much money in the place. "I wish they'd finished the job, so I could just write the whole thing off my taxes and be done with it," he had grumbled.

"But," Mr. Agee observed, "it just occurred to me that there's more than one way to get a tax write-off. If you guys were to just ask him to donate the shell, I'm guessing he'd probably do it in a heartbeat."

Mr. Agee's guess turned out to be quite accurate, and within a few days, the newly-organized ministry held the deed to one completely empty and very sooty house. Another church member, who had done social work in the past, contacted the public defender who was representing the boys in the arson case. Together, they convinced the judge to give all the miscreants community service, which was to be served in renovating the building they had tried to destroy.

The first work party was on a Saturday, with Kelly and Beth as the official leaders. (Don Pillow, who was six-foot-two and had arms like tree limbs, was unofficial escort to the erstwhile arsonists.) Upon their arrival, the girls stood back and surveyed the property.

"Well," said Beth, "what do you think we ought to do first?"

Kelly thought a minute, then picked up a can of spray paint and walked up to the front door. With the practiced hand of a former graffiti artist, she christened the club, "THE JESUS GANG."

"There," she grinned. "Now let's get to work."

19

Opportunity

Some weeks just seem to have nothing but Mondays, Susanna thought as she felt the transmission slip into neutral again, just short of the school parking lot. *When your son is a mechanic, shouldn't you at least be able to count on a car that works?* Thankfully, it was downhill from there all the way to her parking space, so she was able to coast in and leave the problem for later.

Not so with the pile of essays on her desk, their embarrassingly poor grades waiting to be explained to tearful students, angry parents, and frustrated superiors. There was no question that her classes were stocked with some of the hardest cases at Alta Vista High, but Susanna blamed herself for the overall shortcoming. Three months just hadn't proved enough time to make up for the previous four, in which her classes had been all but teacher-less. And now, with final exams just a few weeks away, it looked as though around a dozen students were going to fail outright, with at least that many more just barely scraping by.

Life lately had been like a roller-coaster ride: after church on Sunday, or Bible study on Tuesday night, she was praising the Lord and walking on air. But by the end of a long, grueling week of mountainous paperwork and obstinate pupils, it felt more like slogging uphill through mud. As she often did on mornings like this, Susanna glanced at the copy of Philippians 4:13 she had put on her dashboard. But she was dismayed to see it had somehow gotten torn, and half of it was missing. "I can do all things..." hung rather forlornly from a lone piece of peeling Scotch tape.

The note she found in her mailbox a few minutes later didn't do much to brighten Susanna's day. *Mrs. Kincaid, please come to my office directly after school – Mr. Tyler.* It was *deja vu* at its worst – surely this wasn't the way the story was supposed to go. After all the changes in her life, all the hard work and prayer, was she really going to lose her job anyway?

Regrettably, by the end of the day, that prospect didn't sound nearly as unappealing as it might once have. Larry Feinberg was at his most obstreperous, and Susanna thought Jolene Whitaker was going to have a nervous breakdown over the D on her essay. To top it all off, she had left a job printing on the copier, and returned later to find she had accidentally printed 40 copies of a 12-page document, instead of the 4 she needed. Result: no paper for anyone's copies until someone could get to the office supply, and a very frosty atmosphere in the faculty lounge.

Looking at Principal Tyler's note, which was still lying on her desk, Susanna wondered how she was going to face this meeting. Tears began to roll down her cheeks, which probably would have been the precursor to a waterfall, had not a looming form in her doorway made her dry them quickly. It was Matt Kemp.

"Yes, Matt?" she sniffed, determined to get a hold of herself. "Did you forget something?"

The hulking football player didn't answer immediately; he just shuffled about halfway into the classroom, looking mostly at the floor, and cleared his throat nervously. Susanna came out from behind her desk, and put a hand gently on his arm.

"Is something wrong, Matt?"

"Uh, no.... That is, Mrs. Kincaid, there's something I want to tell you."

"Is this about your essay?" Susanna braced herself for another complaint. She had really thought Matt would be pleased with a C, which for him was an improvement.

"Oh, no, nothing like that. I just wanted to tell you that I went to the FCA meeting today."

"Oh, really? Well, that's great, Matt! You can learn a lot from Mr. Marks." Susanna was well acquainted with Jason Marks, the baseball coach who ran the Fellowship of Christian Athletes chapter in the school. He was a real Christian whose love for Jesus was the only thing that topped his passion for sports.

"Actually," Matt mumbled, "I've been going for a few weeks now. But after what you said in class, it all made sense to me. So this afternoon, I... I prayed with Mr. Marks, and asked Jesus into my heart."

"Oh, Matt...!" That was all Susanna could get out, before the waterfall came down after all. Impulsively, she stood on tiptoes to hug the oversized linebacker around his beefy neck. Suddenly, it all

seemed worth it. Even the miles of red tape, the
Angela Lockes, and the Larry Feinbergs.

Even the meeting with Mr. Tyler, which, she
reminded herself after Matt left, she had yet to face.
But after a talk with her Father, and few minutes
making sure her boss wouldn't know she had been
crying, Susanna felt a lot readier than she had three
months before.

Principal Tyler, however, seemed more nervous,
if anything, as he offered her the same seat in front of
his desk.

"Mrs. Kincaid," he began, "first of all, I want to
say what a marvelous job you have done in the
classroom in these last three months. I'm proud to be
your principal. The whole school is talking about the
great change in you, and about your innovative
teaching methods as well."

Susanna wondered if Mr. Tyler could read the
shock on her face. Could he have somehow confused
her with another teacher? And if he was really that
pleased with her performance, then what was the
meeting about, and why was he so nervous?

"You are probably wondering," he continued, as
though reading her mind, "why I asked to see you. I
must say I wish it was just to give you the
congratulations you deserve. Unfortunately, there is
another issue that has come up, related to your, uh...
religious discourse in the classroom."

"My what?" Susanna felt like she had slipped
into an alternate reality. Her awful teaching results
were great, but there was a problem with the one thing

she had done right! The principal, looking very uncomfortable, took off his spotless glasses and cleaned them again.

"I'm afraid that a certain member of the school board has complained about your, quote, 'proselytizing in the classroom,' unquote. Now let me say," he hastened to add, "that I do not believe for a moment that you intended to do anything of the sort. But as you are still technically on probation, the school board has requested that you make an appearance at their meeting next Wednesday, to explain your recent remarks regarding your faith.

"I believe they simply want your assurance that your personal religious beliefs will be kept out of the classroom, in accordance with school policy, recent court decisions, et cetera."

Susanna just sat for a minute, trying to process what must have happened. The only member of the school board with a child in her class was George Locke – Angela's father. It wasn't hard to guess why he might have it in for her. But making an issue of her sharing the Gospel with troubled teenagers? He was on the mission board of the Presbyterian Church, and taught a Sunday school class to boot!

"Mr. Tyler," Susanna began shakily, "first of all, I want you to know that I have indeed shared my faith with my students, but only in response to their questions. I was not aware that there was any school policy or court decision that forbade such conversations."

"Well then," said Mr. Tyler with a look of relief, "I'm sure there will be no problem. Believe me, Mrs. Kincaid, I'm anxious to put this minor difficulty behind us, and let you get back to the business of teaching. You may not think your students' grades are up to par, but you aren't seeing how the same students are doing in other classes. Besides which, immediate academic achievement isn't the only standard by which I judge my teachers' performance. You are making a positive difference in this school, and as long as that's the case, you'll continue to have my full support."

Susanna's head was awhirl as she drove home that afternoon. Three months ago, she was about to lose her job because she was useless as a teacher. Now, she seemed to be in trouble for the very thing that had transformed her classroom: her faith in Jesus Christ.

Providentially, Tina was coming over that evening, and Susanna could barely wait for her to get in the door, before she poured out the whole crazy story. Her friend sat back, thought a few moments, and then smiled.

"I was just thinking," she said, "about a customer Don had a few years back. This guy would sometimes call him up in the middle of a job and say, 'I have an opportunity for you!' It took Don quite a while to figure out that using the word 'opportunity' was the man's idea of a joke: what he really meant was that there was a problem!

"It made Don mad at first, but then he said to me one day, 'Tina, I've realized that Bill is right. Every problem *is* an opportunity: it's a chance to trust God through it, and let Him be glorified.'

"Now, you and I would think this school board summons is a problem. But from God's perspective, it may be an opportunity – a golden opportunity for the whole school board to hear your testimony."

"But Angela or no Angela," Susanna complained, "I just can't believe Dr. Locke would come out against me on this issue. He's a *deacon*, for crying out loud!"

"The fact that he's a deacon doesn't mean he knows the Lord, Susanna. Religious people are often the most implacable foes of the Gospel: just look at the Apostle Paul, before he met Jesus. But it just might be that the Lord has a Damascus-road experience in store for George Locke, too. Stranger things have happened."

"And continue to happen," Susanna agreed. "The next thing I expect to see is...."

She paused. What a crazy thought.

"What?"

"Oh, nothing. Just thinking about someone else who needs the Lord. But I really don't expect to ever see him again."

20

Help Wanted

"This is gonna blow your mind, Mr. K." Phil shook his head as he counted his newspaper-clad fee, as though he himself didn't quite believe the report he was about to deliver.

"I knew it must be something important, for you to ask for a meeting somewhere other than 'the usual place.'" Ross tried without success to keep the sarcasm out of his voice, but Phil didn't seem to notice.

"Too many people at the diner this time of day," he explained. "Nobody at this park at lunch time but the pigeons. It's a lot of trouble to bug a pigeon – hardly anyone would bother."

Ross would have liked to think that last observation was a joke, but he knew Phil too well to believe that. "So what's the big news?" he prompted.

"Your ex-wife apparently went and got religion."

"You're kidding."

"No mistake," Phil asserted. "Information comes from good, reliable sources. You were right about the singing at the house the other night: she was hosting a Bible study."

Ross felt as though the sun had just risen in the west. Susanna and religion, in the same sentence even? The most religious thing he had ever heard her say was "good heavens!" But emotional trauma made people do strange things.

"What kind of religion are we talking about?" he asked apprehensively. "I mean, does it seem like she's gone off the deep end?"

"Could be," Phil conceded. "It's hard to get much information on the church she's joined. They're really new – in fact, they hold their Sunday meetings in an auto parts store. I have heard the word 'cult' used, but you have to take that with a grain of salt. Some people think you've joined a cult if you just change your hair style."

Ross winced. He wasn't sure if the news was getting better, or worse.

"There's more," Phil said, "and I really don't know what to think about this part. She got on probation at her teaching job back in January, right around the time she started going to this church. Now they've put her on the school board agenda, and the rumor is that it's because someone has complained about her preaching in the classroom."

"Preaching? Are you going to tell me that Susanna's a preacher now?"

Phil shrugged. "Like I said, it's a rumor. But with the lawsuit-crazy climate these days, students are getting sent to the principal's office for praying over lunch. I mean, these legal beagles are the definition of paranoid."

Ross was too worried to notice the almost laughable irony of that statement, coming from a man who literally wore a bulletproof vest to bed. "I need to know what happens at that school board meeting," he said firmly. "Can you find out for me?"

Phil snorted. "Can Joe Montana throw a spiral? Just leave it to me, Mr. K."

Had Ross been on speaking terms with God, he'd have thanked Him for this nutty private eye. Where Phil got the kind of information he did was a mystery that Ross didn't dare inquire into, knowing he'd just get a long lecture on the security of sources and the extreme danger of the business.

Actually, Ross had begun to catch a little of the spy-novel spirit himself. Having a secret identity made him feel strangely powerful – like he was looking at life through a two-way mirror, seeing without being observed. His second meeting with Chuck, to approve the estimate, had passed without incident, and this afternoon he was heading back to the garage to pick up the renovated truck. This time he planned to arrive deliberately early, in hopes of picking up some conversation while waiting around in the shop. If the timing seemed right, he was ready to make his next move.

"Afternoon, Mr. Morton!" The greeting came from under a car, but Ross recognized the voice of Chuck's cheerful co-worker, David. He had noticed the young mechanic on previous visits; his frequent, happy whistling reminded Ross of Jacob.

"Chuck's on a parts run right now," David explained, emerging from beneath the chassis. "We weren't expecting you until later."

"Oh, I must have written down the wrong time," Ross lied. "But that's okay, I don't have to be anywhere for a few hours. I'll just hang around here and wait for him to come back."

"There's free coffee in the waiting room," David offered. "Though confidentially," he added in a lower tone, "it's pretty much indistinguishable from the transmission fluid."

"Thanks for the warning," Ross smiled, settling into a chair near Chuck's desk. "I'll just wait over here, if you don't mind. I like to be near where the action is."

"You sound just like Chuck," David laughed. Ross tensed briefly, but realized David had no idea what he was saying. "So have you worked here long?" he asked casually.

"No, only about six months," David replied, his voice slightly muffled as he slid back under the car. "Chuck's been here going on three years. He's a really good mechanic – makes me look like an amateur, to tell you the truth."

"Yeah, I can tell he's got talent. Guess he probably has his eye on his own shop one day, huh?"

David's head reappeared, and he glanced toward the office with a worried look. "Well, that might be," he agreed quietly. "But of course, it's not the sort of thing we talk about around here."

"Oh, right, of course. But I'm sure your boss knows he can't keep good talent for nothing. A young man's got to get ahead, especially if he has a family to support."

"Well, Chuck's not married, but he does want to get ahead, no doubt about it. He's got a little too much drive, if you ask me. Which no one did, I guess." He stopped and smiled. "I talk too much."

Ross ignored his self-criticism, hoping the young man's scruples wouldn't shut off the flow of information. "I don't see anything wrong with ambition," he opined. "It's what makes things happen in this world."

"Can't argue with that," David agreed. "Of course, that includes both good and bad things. And sometimes even the good things aren't so good, in the long run."

"You'll have to explain that one."

With the grunt of a final tightening stroke, David emerged and wiped his hands. "Well, Napoleon certainly was ambitious. So were Hitler, and Stalin, and Mao, and they all looked pretty good for a while. But in the end, they destroyed their countries, and some of them their own lives, even."

"Yeah, but most of those guys were nuts. Or at least really, really evil."

David shrugged. "Who's to say? What they did probably made sense to them. Without a supreme moral authority, right and wrong are just a matter of opinion."

This guy was sounding more like Jacob all the time. Ross hesitated to go down the religious road, but guessed it might lead somewhere useful. "So let me guess," he ventured. "You *do* believe in absolute right and wrong."

"Absolutely," David grinned.

"And let me further guess that you believe those absolutes are found...."

"In the Bible," David finished. "But how did you know?"

"Experience," Ross sighed. "You're not the first outspoken Christian I've met."

David clocked out and began scrubbing his hands with a gritty cleaner. "I gather your previous experiences haven't been altogether pleasant?"

"I wouldn't say that, exactly," Ross shrugged. "In fact, one of the nicest guys I ever met was a Christian. Trouble was, he was Jewish, and his family literally disowned him for believing in Jesus. He died without ever getting to see his parents again."

"Wow." David sat down and unwrapped a granola bar. "You don't hear about that kind of commitment every day. At least, not in this country. But you know, Jesus warned his followers to expect things like that to happen to them. He said He would divide families, and anyone who loved brother, sister, or parents more than Him, wasn't worthy to be his disciple."

"That's pretty heavy stuff," Ross observed.

"So is life. People are willing to make those kinds of sacrifices for what they want. The trouble is, they don't really believe God really means what He says in his word. They'll tell you they want to go to Heaven, but they'll hardly cross the street to do anything about it, let alone come to Jesus and have their life turned upside down. Or rather," he corrected, "right side up."

"Guess it all depends on your point of view," Ross smiled. "But I find yours very interesting. You go to church around here?"

"Actually, I'm sort of between churches right now. I'm planning to check out the one Chuck's mom and sister go to this Sunday. I've already been to their Bible study, and it was great."

Ross's heart rate went up, but he kept his voice casual. "Oh, so is Chuck's family religious too?"

David laughed as he munched his granola bar. "I certainly hope not! Religion never saved anyone. But if you mean, are they Christians, yes – except for Chuck himself, that is. I think he's more like you: somewhere between interested and cynical."

"Who's cynical?" Chuck demanded, walking in at just that moment.

"Oh, nobody," David replied, looking at the ceiling. "We were just discussing some theoretical mechanic, who wants to make a lot of money, and wishes God would stop bugging him."

"Don't pay any attention to this clown, Mr. Morton," Chuck advised. "He talks too much."

"So he was telling me," Ross chuckled. "But I can tell you two work well together. In fact, I have a proposition for you." He dropped his voice.

"How would you both like to work for me?"

21

Into The Lions' Den

Ever since the family meal had been re-instituted as a tradition in the Kincaid home, it hadn't once been anything like dull, or even quiet. If Susanna and Kelly weren't chattering excitedly about everything the Lord had done that day, they were (with varying degrees of love and tact) trying their best to get Chuck to see the light.

Although he could have done without the preaching, Chuck couldn't help but enjoy the feeling of being a family once again. In bygone days, he could have said that the shop had burned to the ground that afternoon, and gotten nothing more than a glazed stare from his mother and a "so what?" look from his sister. Now, they both listened with interest to everything he said, even things that weren't all that interesting.

On this particular evening, however, the atmosphere was quite different, as it was the night of the school board meeting. Susanna barely touched her food, and even Kelly wasn't going on incessantly about her "gang" and their crazy construction project.

Chuck really couldn't understand why his mother was so worked up about the meeting. "It's just bureaucracy, Mom," he had tried to reassure her. "They don't want to be sued, so they're making sure you don't get them in legal trouble."

But she seemed determined to make a big deal out of it, and even went a whole day without eating, which had something to do with being prepared. (Chuck would later learn that this was called "fasting" – apparently an important word to know if you wanted to sound interested in Christianity.)

The whole affair had been so obviously weighing on her mind, that Chuck had decided it would be best not to tell her about Roger Morton's strange offer. He and David had discussed it at length, and agreed to keep it between themselves for at least two of the three weeks the mysterious investor had given them to think it over.

Chuck had racked his brain day and night for the last five days, trying to exhaust every possibility that this whole thing could be some kind of scam. One thing Chuck had learned the hard way was that if something seems too good to be true, it probably is.

As a kid, he had scraped together six weeks' allowance to send away for a bag of "very old, unsorted coins from the U.S. Mint." His heart racing and his imagination full of rare coins worth hundreds, he had opened the box to find roughly $17 worth of rather dirty pennies, dimes, and nickels. Outraged, he had taken both the goods and the newspaper ad to his social studies teacher, who carefully explained the cruel legalities of advertising and "buyer beware."

The trouble was, no matter how hard he looked, Chuck couldn't find anything to "beware" of in this very much too-good-to-be-true deal. According to Morton, he had come to California looking for investment opportunities. A friend of his, who owned a small but successful garage that specialized in import cars, was retiring, and looking to sell the business. Morton intended to buy it, and hire Chuck and David to run it, eventually returning to Texas, where he made his permanent home.

Morton claimed he had bought the truck specifically to use it as a test, and that Chuck was the first mechanic to correctly diagnose the problem and give him a fair and thorough estimate for the repair. (Although it did seem a little strange to Chuck that he had made the offer without actually driving the vehicle to make sure it was fixed.)

"Besides," he had said, "I didn't get where I am in business by being a poor judge of human capital. I knew from the minute I saw you two that you were the guys for the job."

It all sounded like something out of a Charles Dickens novel. But if the whole thing was somehow a scam, then where was the catch? Both David and Chuck had visited the shop Morton said he was buying, and found it exactly as described. He hadn't asked them to invest a penny. All they had to do was give Rocky Philips notice (which would be a pure pleasure to Chuck), and show up ready to work on June 1st, the day after the closing. David was just about ready to believe it was a gift from God, while Chuck was still trying to convince himself that anyone could be this lucky.

But tonight, he was determined to put aside his own mental wranglings and offer his mom some support. The meeting was a closed session, so he and Kelly weren't allowed to go in, but they agreed to drive her to the administration building and wait outside. Kelly assured her mom she'd be praying the whole time, and Chuck surprised them both by promising to add his own prayers, too, "for what it's worth."

Thunder was rumbling overhead when they left the house, and by the time they reached the school parking lot, the building was almost obscured by the downpour. Susanna gave a brave smile to her children before stepping out with her umbrella into the deluge. Even though she didn't put much stock in the efficacy of Chuck's prayers, it felt good to have him there with her. More reassuring still was the hand of her Heavenly Father, which she consciously took hold of in her heart as she walked into the large, echoing vestibule.

"Mrs. Kincaid?" The receptionist peered over a thick stack of files, which she seemed to be sorting without much pleasure.

"That's me!" Susanna answered brightly, but the woman's expression remained as glum as ever.

"Have a seat, please; you'll be called shortly."

Susanna settled down in one of the overly-soft waiting room chairs, and tried to improve the time: first by reading the pocket New Testament she always carried, then by praying. Finding herself unable to concentrate on either, she wound up simply watching the minute hand on the wall clock make its unhurried circuit around the ornate face. As it eventually approached its starting position, Susanna began to wonder just how long "shortly" might turn out to be. Just then, a door opened and she heard her name called again. With a final prayer for wisdom, Susanna took a deep breath and entered the school board meeting room.

At the end of the long conference-room table sat the mild-mannered chairman, Mr. Daniel, one of only two people in the room Susanna knew by sight. The other, of course, was George Locke, who sat nearest Susanna on the right side. His physical appearance certainly didn't intimidate; he was balding, slightly overweight, and wore glasses. But he had a reputation as a man who got what he wanted – a reputation that was usually enough to keep sensible people from getting in his way.

The chairman invited her to sit down, and opened with pleasantries, but quickly gave the floor to Dr. Locke, who turned a page on the yellow legal pad before him and adjusted his bifocals.

"Mrs. Kincaid," he began, "is it true that you have, for several years, habitually abused both alcohol and prescription medications?"

Susanna was dumbstruck. Wasn't this meeting supposed to be about her "proselytizing in the classroom"? She cast a questioning glance at Mr. Daniel, but he only stared back impassively.

"Well, yes... up until recently," she stammered. "But you must understand that there have been significant changes in my life...."

"And is it also true," Dr. Locke interrupted, "that you were a patient of a certain Dr. Harvey Strait – the same Dr. Strait who was recently convicted on multiple drug-related charges, and sentenced to five years in prison?"

Susanna felt her pulse rising, and she struggled to keep her voice even. "Yes, but once again, I'd like to explain what has happened to me since...."

"Isn't it also true," Dr. Locke continued, "that your daughter Kelly was involved with a known heroin dealer earlier this year? And that she was in the car that he crashed while under the influence, resulting in the death of another girl?"

Fearing she was about to lose control of her emotions, Susanna simply nodded. A low rumble of thunder seemed to accentuate the silence. She couldn't believe that the rest of the school board, especially Mr. Daniel, just sat there and said nothing. Was this even legal? Dr. Locke turned another page on his pad and sighed.

"We are aware, Mrs. Kincaid, of the personal problems you've had to cope with since your divorce. Several complaints against you in the past have been overlooked, in the hope of your eventual... how should I put it? Recovery? In any case...."

"But I *have* recovered...." Susanna's voice was cracked, and she had to brush away a tear.

"In any case," repeated Dr. Locke with more emphasis, "what we seem to have now is a compounding of these issues, with your lately acquired interest in religion. How you deal with your own private struggles is your own business, of course – at least until such time as your personal choices impact your job performance to an unacceptable degree. But when you lecture the students on religion, and lead them to believe that some sort of faith experience can nullify the effects of drugs and alcohol.... Mrs. Kincaid, I put it to you that this is a very dangerous message, and one which we cannot tolerate being taught to our children."

Susanna knew that the battle was lost. As soon as she opened her mouth, she would burst into tears. She would never be able to explain, or make the school board understand. All the work and prayer of the last three months would go for nothing. *Where are you, Father?*

Suddenly, there was an enormous peal of thunder, that literally made the whole room jump. All the lights immediately went out.

"Don't worry, the backup generator will kick in momentarily." The voice was that of Mr. Daniel, calm and reassuring as always. The board waited... and waited. And Susanna prayed.

"What is going on, Bruce?" Dr. Locke's voice was highly irritated. "We spent thousands on that backup power system – how can it not be working?"

"I have no idea," the chairman replied, the bafflement evident in his voice. "But obviously we can't just sit here in the dark." Feeling his way around to a nearby cabinet, he managed to locate a flashlight, which looked like the sun after minutes of inky gloom.

"Since this was the last item on the agenda," suggested Mr. Daniel, "I move we postpone further discussion until the next board meeting in two weeks, which will also be the last of the school year. Mrs. Kincaid, will you be able to appear before the board again at that time?"

"Yes, sir," Susanna managed.

"Very well then. All in favor?"

The nearly unanimous "aye" was missing only one voice, as far as Susanna could tell – Dr. Locke's. As they all filed out in the narrow flashlight beam, he got close enough to Susanna to speak so only she could hear.

"Do yourself a favor, Mrs. Kincaid – find another job."

Not even that parting growl could steal the joy that was beginning to rise again in Susanna's heart. The Hand that once held lions' mouths tightly shut still had her hand firmly in His grasp.

22

Big Enough God

"Hello, no one is available to take your call. Please leave a message after the beep." Beth groaned as she hung up the phone. "Still no answer at Matt Kemp's house. Are you about ready for a break?"

Kelly, who had just wrapped up her own phone call, stood up and stretched. "Yeah, I guess. I keep thinking I'm going to wake up and realize that all this is just some crazy dream."

Beth had to agree: the past two weeks had gone by in a blur. First there was the late-night phone call from an almost incoherent Kelly, raging about how her mom had just been "ambushed" by the school board. An emergency prayer meeting at the Kincaids' house had settled things down a bit. Pastor Grayson managed to get everyone's focus off George Locke, and back onto Jesus.

"Think about how powerfully He intervened on your behalf," the pastor admonished. "The board could have voted right then, and it would all have been over. Somehow, He still has a plan for you there, Susanna."

Just what that plan might be seemed like anyone's guess at the time. Susanna steadfastly maintained that there was no way she could go into that meeting alone again. And yet there seemed to be no way around it, apart from simply resigning – the meeting was closed, and that was that.

Then, two days and many prayers later, came a very strange phone call. The man identified himself as a lawyer with the American Civil Rights Organization – a group that was better known for attacking religious freedom than defending it. Nonetheless, on the strength of "an anonymous report" about the school board meeting, he had called to offer some free advice.

"Your local school board statute doesn't require closed sessions for personnel matters," he explained. "They are closed by default, but if the employee in question formally requests it, he or she *must* be given a public hearing. You need to demand a public hearing, and invite as many people as you can. This sort of thing can attract a lot of publicity, which should work in your favor."

Susanna was profoundly grateful for this answer to prayer (and told the lawyer so, much to his embarrassment), but she had some misgivings at first. Getting her family and church to come and support her was one thing, but trying to attract publicity? That was something altogether different, especially for such a private person as Susanna had always been.

Another prayer meeting was called, but the prayers were soon interrupted (not to mention rendered irrelevant) by several more phone calls. Somehow, the local TV station had already gotten wind of the situation, and wanted to do an interview. Other news outlets soon followed suit, but the coverage wasn't wholly sympathetic.

Organized opposition quickly appeared in the form of a local atheist league, which had been fighting for several years to have the opening prayer removed from the city council meetings. Dr. Locke, who was also on the city council, and had fought to keep the prayer, now found himself in the embarrassing position of being on the same side with the atheists. With a school board election coming up, some groups sought to make the whole affair a political issue, and even floated the idea of running Susanna as a candidate. (This notion she appreciatively, but very firmly quashed.)

Her church and family generally agreed, however, that it would be a good idea to have as many of Susanna's supporters at the meeting as possible. If nothing else, it was an opportunity to share the Gospel with everyone in attendance. This Susanna had every intention of doing, whether it got her fired in the end or not.

And so was born the "Kincaid Phone Bank" – a moniker jokingly coined by Kelly. For the last three evenings, she and Beth had been calling just about everyone they could think of, making sure they knew the time and place of the meeting.

It was a totally new experience for both girls, but good practice, Beth observed, for the future of their inner-city outreach. Even the materials needed for renovation of the house had quickly exhausted their meager resources, and further work was on hold, pending some sort of fundraising effort. Between The Jesus Gang, organizing for the school board meeting, and her regular load of college classes, Beth didn't know whether she was coming or going.

And then, in the middle of everything, was Chuck. He and Beth had finally been introduced at the first emergency prayer meeting. Chuck didn't participate, Beth noticed, but he didn't walk out either. He was very supportive of his mother, and didn't even complain when an increasingly hectic household schedule translated to fewer hot meals and less regular laundry service. A couple of times, he spelled one or the other of the girls in the phone bank. Despite the often-annoying nature of the work, he was always respectful, and even a little charming.

Beth wasn't long in finding out from Kelly that Chuck wasn't saved... yet. "He really has seemed a lot more open in the past few weeks," Kelly had shared hopefully. "Please keep praying for him."

The really surprising moment for both girls had come that very evening, though, when Chuck himself had asked them to pray. "I'm considering what looks like a really good job offer," he explained. "I haven't told Mom yet, because I don't want to disappoint or worry her right now. But I figure it can't hurt for you guys to put in a word for me with... you know, the Lord."

Beth had been thinking about the incident throughout the evening's tedious work. "So what did you make of Chuck's prayer request?" she asked Kelly in a low voice, as they fixed up a bowl of snack mix.

Kelly's brow furrowed. "I honestly don't know, Beth," she replied. "Chuck was so opposed to the

Gospel at first, but everything seemed to change about the time...."

Beth suddenly had a sinking feeling. "About the time he met me? You don't think...."

"What's up, ladies?" Chuck's jaunty frame filled the kitchen doorway. "Secret meeting?"

"More like a secret snack," Beth blushed. "Want some Chex mix?"

"Sure – just don't put any walnuts in it. David asked if he could drop by later, so of course I said yes."

"Chuck!" Kelly moaned. "How are we going to finish our calls tonight?"

"No sweat, sis," Chuck grinned. "I'll take over your phone, and you and your suitor can take a moonlit walk."

Now it was Kelly's turn to blush, a much deeper shade of red. "He's not a suitor! And you know I don't do moonlit walks these days, anyway."

"Sure, whatever," Chuck laughed. "Though I'll never understand how you expect to quit dating, and still find a man."

"I haven't quit dating," Kelly corrected. "I'm just not dating boys who aren't Christians, that's all."

"Which, according to your definition of 'Christian,' leaves...?"

"Lots of guys!" Kelly insisted. "I just don't happen to know more than... a few of them yet," she added more quietly.

"I think the number you were looking for is 'one,'" Chuck teased as he walked off, munching snack mix.

True to her word, Kelly didn't go for a moonlit walk that evening, but of course David didn't ask. He and Kelly did have a long talk on the porch, during which he was thoroughly briefed on all her supposedly-secret plans for The Jesus Gang. Their call list complete, Beth and Chuck joined the duo outside, finished off the snack mix, and then sat watching the stars come out.

"I never used to notice how beautiful they are," Kelly mused softly.

"You know," David said, "when I was a little boy, I used to get scared looking into the night sky, thinking how big God must be to have made all that. I didn't like to think about going to Heaven and meeting God – it actually made me dizzy.'

"So what did you do?" Kelly prompted.

"I told my dad how I felt, and he set me on his lap, and said, 'Davy, I'm a lot bigger than you, but you're not scared of me. Why is that?'"

"'I guess it's because you love me,' I said. 'Well,' he said, 'God's a *lot* bigger than me, but I'm not scared of Him, because He's my Father, and He loves me just like I love you. And He's your Father too, Davy, and He loves you even more than I do. Don't ever be scared to come to Him. Just be thankful that He's big enough to save us.' I think about that night every time I look at the stars."

"What a great memory to have," Beth said quietly.

"Yeah, that must be nice," Chuck commented, letting more bitterness creep into his voice than he intended. He got up with a stretch and a yawn.

"I'd better turn in, guys – got a big day tomorrow. Beth, I really enjoyed cold calling with you tonight, and that's saying something. I hired on with a telemarketing company one summer and lasted all of six hours."

"So that's where you got your experience," Beth chuckled. "Well I enjoyed it too, and thanks for helping out."

The dim light of the citronella lamps caught Chuck's winsome smile. "Maybe we can do it again some time?"

Beth smiled too, at the deliberately unromantic joke, but still found her heart skipped a beat.

"Maybe," she said. "We'll see."

23
Take No Thought

"Elsewhere tonight, a local high school history teacher will appear before the school board, to answer allegations of substance abuse, and religious proselytizing in the classroom."

Wiping the shaving cream off his face, Ross stepped out of the bathroom and turned up the TV volume.

"Susanna Kincaid," continued the anchor, "has been a teacher at Alta Vista High School for over ten years. Until just a few weeks ago, her career was unnoticed and unremarkable. But tonight, she stands at the center of a raging controversy, with implications ranging from the religious to the political."

The news program cut to an interview shot with Susanna, and Ross sat down on the bed. There she was, after all these years. She had certainly aged better than he had. And although she was clearly nervous, she also looked... happy, somehow.

"I don't think of myself as an evangelist," Susanna was saying. "At least, not any more than any other Christian. I love teaching history, and I'd like to keep doing it. But when someone asks me about the change in my life – whether that's a student, or... or the chairman of the school board – I'm going to tell them it's Jesus."

Jesus. So it was true. To hear the woman he had lived with for thirteen years say that name with such obvious reverence and sincerity was a strange experience for Ross. Unnerving, even. It had been a lot easier to picture her as a drug addict; at least a wrecked life was one thing they'd have in common. But now – how would they ever relate? She might as well be on another planet.

The news anchor didn't show any more of the interview with Susanna; apparently he considered a harangue by the leader of the atheist group more interesting. "It couldn't be more obvious that the law is on our side," the woman smugly asserted. "We are confident that the school board will make the right decision this evening, and keep religion out of our classrooms."

Ross chuckled to himself as he thought about how mad that lady was going to be after tonight. He hadn't felt exhilaration like this since he moved a whole bank project across a four-lane highway, and did a greedy real-estate broker out of $3 million.

Of course, he had to privately admit that he couldn't have pulled this one off without help from Phil and his mysterious sources. But once he had the information he needed, it was just another business deal – and making deals was one thing Ross was good at. A well-placed phone call here, a little campaign contribution there, and everything was going according to plan.

As if on cue, the phone rang just then. It was a call he'd been expecting, from his covertly hired civil rights attorney.

"Did you take care of it?" he asked, without bothering to say hello.

"Well... yes and no," came the hesitant reply.

"What do you mean, yes and no?" Ross yelled. "Did you tell her what to say, or not?"

"Calm down, Mr. Morton. I called Mrs. Kincaid, just as you requested, and I explained to her that everything had been arranged. I told her that all she had to do was keep quiet at the hearing, and she'd not only keep her job, she'd be promoted."

"And? What are you trying to say – that she turned you down?"

"She said she'd pray about it."

Ross sank onto the bed again. "You're kidding."

"I wish I were. Mr. Morton, I don't know how much experience you have with religious people, but I can tell you that they often act this way – especially Christians. They just don't do things according to their own best interests."

Ross felt stunned as he hung up the phone. He had moved half the county to get everything fixed for Susanna, and all she could say was that she'd pray about it?

Had he known the answer to those prayers, which was coming through in his old living room at that very moment, Ross would have been even more disturbed. As the murmur of supplication died down, Tina Pillow reached for her Bible, and effortlessly turned to the passage that the Lord had just spoken to her spirit.

"But when they deliver you up, take no thought how or what ye shall speak: for it shall be given you in that same hour what ye shall speak. For it is not ye that speak, but the Spirit of your Father which speaketh in you."

The holy hush over the room was almost palpable. After a long and beautiful silence that was filled with God's presence, Beth began to sing, and the others softly joined in.

Have thine own way, Lord, have thine own way
Hold o'er my being, absolute sway
Fill with thy Spirit, till all shall see
Christ only, always, living in me.

Susanna let out a joyful, contented sigh as she rose from her knees. "I think we're ready, ladies. Shall we go?"

24

Permission To Speak

"Excuse me, but are those seats taken?"

"Yes, they are – sorry." Chuck sighed as he gave the answer for what seemed like the twentieth time that evening. In anticipation of an unusually large crowd of spectators, the school board meeting had been moved to City Hall. Even that venue, however, proved insufficient to accommodate the ever-growing throng of supporters, opponents, and curious onlookers. No one could remember seeing this many TV cameras in town since a double murder trial in the sixties.

Craning his neck to find a gap in the wall of humanity, Chuck finally caught sight of Susanna, Kelly, and Beth, squeezing their way to the front.

"Where in the world have you guys been?" Chuck asked impatiently. "The meeting starts in five minutes!"

"I know, honey." Susanna smiled, and patted his hand as she sat down. "Don't worry, everything is going to be fine."

"Fine?" Chuck was genuinely confused. "You said yourself that the last time you faced these guys, you almost came unglued. But now that it's blown up into a federal case, with half the city watching, you're as cool as a cucumber. Do you know something I don't?"

"You could say that," Susanna mused. "Or, more accurately, I know *Someone* you don't, although I hope you'll get to meet Him soon."

Chuck looked at Kelly, then at Beth, and found them both wearing the same crazy smile as his mother. *They must all be bananas*, he decided. *I'd better be careful not to overdose on this religion thing. If Mom loses her job, which she probably will, I'm going to need all my wits to support the family.*

The meeting, as it turned out, was fifteen minutes late starting, as it took that long to settle the crowd, and get all the reporters and their cameras in position. Mr. Daniel, who seemed very ill at ease, opened the proceedings with rather more than the usual formality, almost as though he were presiding over a court case instead of a school board meeting.

"Now as to the matter for which, uh, I believe most of you are here... well, I'm going to let Mrs. Osborne introduce this item on the agenda."

A murmur of surprise went through the audience at this announcement. Janet Osborne was the wife of a state senator, and the only school board member with arguably more clout than Dr. Locke. However, she was only on the board for political reasons, and rarely even attended meetings, let alone took an active hand in affairs.

"Mrs. Kincaid," she began, "first of all, I'd like to apologize, on behalf of the school board, for the unnecessary trouble, and invasion of your privacy to which you've been subjected over the last couple of weeks." A couple of the TV cameras panned to Dr.

Locke, who was looking down at his notepad with an expression of grim resignation.

"Some of the board members have privately reviewed your record," Mrs. Osborne continued, "and we have concluded that your performance as a teacher is more than satisfactory. We realize it was not your intention to discuss religion in the classroom in an inappropriate manner. Therefore, I would like to move at this time...."

"Excuse me?" Susanna stood up, and all the TV cameras were on her instantly. Janet Osborne looked completely shocked, and exchanged questioning looks with George Locke.

"Mrs. Kincaid," Dr. Locke attempted, "it really isn't necessary for you to...."

"Excuse me, Dr. Locke," Susanna interrupted, "but I believe this meeting was made public at my request. I understand that I have a right to address the board before any motion is made concerning my employment. Is that correct?"

"Uh, yes," Dr. Locke stammered. "But I don't think you understand...."

"I understand that I need to set the record straight on a few things, sir, with all due respect."

With a helpless shrug, the doctor gestured to her to continue.

"First of all, Mrs. Osborne, you said that my record was satisfactory. Well, it's kind of you to say so, but I know it's not the case."

Another murmur of disbelief went through the crowd. In the back row, a man with a scarred face, who had been watching intently, flinched as though he had been hit.

"Up until January of this year," Susanna continued, "I was a pathetic excuse for a teacher. I was a hopeless alcoholic, and hooked on prescription medications to boot. Many days I didn't teach at all – I just sat at my desk while my students watched movies. I was a terrible example to them, choosing escape from my problems, instead of reaching out for the answer."

"Then, one night about four months ago, I got to the end of my rope. I was literally ready to take my own life, and leave my children to pick up the pieces. But by God's grace, He stopped me in my tracks, and sent me a friend, who introduced me to Jesus Christ."

Mrs. Osborne cleared her throat. "Ah, Mrs. Kincaid, this is hardly the time or the place...."

"Since that time," Susanna pressed on, "my life has been completely different. I am completely off both drugs and alcohol. I have rediscovered my love of teaching, and my love for my students. I care about every one of them, and want the best for them in this world, and in the one I believe is coming.

As a public school teacher, I realize that it isn't my job to teach my students about God. But as their friend, and as a follower of Jesus Christ, I can and must take every opportunity to point them to the answer I have found.

"I do not pretend that my faith in Jesus has completely reversed the damage I did, either to my health, my family, or my students. But by God's grace, I intend to make every day I have left count. If you see fit to allow me to continue to do that as a history teacher at Alta Vista High School, I will be grateful. If not, I will still be grateful, because I have found the purpose of life, and nothing can take that away from me."

Susanna sat down, and for a few very long seconds, the whole room was silent. Then, Mrs. Osborne slowly shook her head.

"Mrs. Kincaid, I must say that I'm very disturbed by your remarks. Naturally, everyone is glad you have succeeded in getting your life back together, but the public schools, and school board meetings, are not appropriate venues to discuss private religious faith. This board can't possibly condone your determination to continue using your position for such activities. Therefore, I must regretfully change the motion I was about to propose." She glanced over at Dr. Locke, but he was looking down again.

"I must move," she continued, "that the board terminate Mrs. Kincaid's contract, with immediate effect, under the provisions of section twenty-one, which pertains to conduct potentially incurring liability for the school district."

Susanna was disappointed when Mr. Daniel seconded the motion – though it was clearly with some hesitation. Years ago, as a high school principal, he had been the one to offer Susanna her first teaching position.

One by one, the board members registered their votes on the city council's electronic board, but everyone already knew what the tally would be. Susanna would receive support from Dr. Coates (a former Baptist missionary, absent the night of the grilling) and Rita Macklin, who wasn't religious, but was an outspoken proponent of free speech rights. Dr. Locke would cast the deciding vote, and that would of course be....

But nothing was lit yet next to his name. He just sat there, still not looking up, an inscrutably serious expression on his face.

Mr. Daniel looked at him and raised an eyebrow. "George?"

Slowly, the doctor reached underneath the table – and lit the red light for "no."

For a moment, there was a silent pause of disbelief.

Then, there was pandemonium. Spectators cheered their support, or roared their protest. Susanna hugged Chuck, then Kelly and Beth at once. Journalists converged to get a statement. Mr. Daniel pounded his gavel fruitlessly, then finally gave up and adjourned the meeting. Mrs. Osborne had some angry words for Dr. Locke, which no one else could hear over the din.

Susanna, seeing the doctor about to leave, pressed her way through the knot of reporters to shake his hand. "I want to thank you, sir," she said. "I know that was not an easy decision."

"Don't thank me," he replied, without any trace of animosity. "I may never know why I pushed that button. My vote may have saved your job for now, but it will probably end my political career. They'll eventually find a way to get rid of you too, I'm sure. But for what it's worth, Mrs. Kincaid, I believe you are the most remarkable woman I have ever met."

"It's Jesus that's remarkable, Dr. Locke," Susanna replied. "And at the hearing we're all headed to, his is the only vote that matters."

"Good point," agreed the doctor, with just a hint of a smile. "Keep preaching it while you can."

"By his grace, I will," Susanna promised. "With every breath."

25

Mr. Morton's Dinner Party

During Ross's high school days, he once spent a summer selling kitchen knives door-to-door with an older, and far more experienced partner by the name of Gary Still. This fast-talking salesman, whose personal appearance was always immaculate, was forever admonishing Ross to comb his hair, tie his shoe, button his collar, etc. By the time they parted ways in September, Ross was heartily sick of both Gary's housewife-tuned sales pitch and his personal mantra: "You never get a second chance to make a first impression!"

On this particular evening, however, Ross almost wished that he knew how to reach Gary, so he could prove to him that his favorite rule had at least one exception. He was about to make a second "first impression" with the woman he had married and divorced, and he was determined to make it a good one.

The day after the school board meeting, Ross had gotten the call he was expecting from Chuck: he and David were both in. He smiled when he thought about it – at least he could count on Chuck to "act in his own best interests." That boy reminded him more of himself every day.

Susanna, on the other hand, had changed beyond recognition as far as Ross was concerned. The Susanna he knew wouldn't even tell her friends when she was pregnant, until the fact became too obvious to hide. Could the same woman actually stand up in a school board meeting, and confess to alcoholism and drug addiction, with the TV cameras broadcasting every word?

With all his misgivings, Ross was intensely curious about Susanna, and also about Kelly, who had apparently undergone a metamorphosis of her own. He was very pleased when they accepted his invitation, via Chuck, to attend the Friday night dinner party celebrating their new business venture. Utilizing his "two-way mirror" powers, Ross had thrown in the added incentive of holding the party at the Mongolian Grill, which he knew was one of Susanna's favorite restaurants. Of course, he had to be careful not to overdo it and "blow his cover," as Phil had put it. It would be a very tricky balancing act, but Ross was sure that if anyone could pull it off, he could.

As the minutes ticked by toward the appointed time, each one slower than the last, Ross divided his nervous glances between his watch, and the door where his ex-wife, son, and daughter would appear at any moment. And then – there they were. Plastering on his most polite poker face, Ross stood to meet the "strangers."

Chuck made the presentations, unaware of the extreme irony of introducing his mother to his father. Ross watched Susanna's and Kelly's faces closely for any sign of recognition, and inwardly breathed a sigh of relief when he found none. This was it at last: a chance to rebuild himself, literally from scratch, in the eyes of the people he had hurt so badly a decade ago. David and his family had somehow been delayed, so it seemed that fate was already on his side, giving him a chance to break the ice.

"So, Mrs. Kincaid," he offered, as they sampled the hors d'oeuvres, "I hear you've become quite the local celebrity of late. Thinking of running for office, perhaps?"

Susanna blushed and laughed at the same time. "I'm just thankful to still have the job I started with. I'm certainly not cut out for politics."

"Oh, I don't know about that," Ross demurred. "I thought that speech you gave was quite impressive."

"If you really knew me, Mr. Morton, you'd know that *wasn't* me talking."

Chuck cleared his throat meaningfully. "What Mom means is that she's passionate about teaching and about her faith – but she hates the limelight."

"Well, I can certainly respect that. I'm more or less indifferent to fame, myself. And, while I do prefer wealth to poverty, I've learned that money isn't everything, either."

"So what is it that you do value, then, Mr. Morton?" asked Susanna with a smile.

"People," Ross replied without hesitation. "I didn't always realize it, but I've come to believe that relationships are the most important things in life."

"So do you have family?" The question, coming from a completely innocent Kelly, made something catch in Ross's throat, and he had to clear it before replying.

"No, nobody. Only child, parents dead, never married."

"Why not?"

"Too busy with business, I guess," he smiled sadly.

"Well, you seem to have done pretty well for yourself," Chuck observed. "Not many people could take a trip out to California and buy an auto repair shop, just like that."

"Making money isn't actually as hard as most people think," Ross said. "Once you get the right connections, it kind of starts a chain reaction, and the more you have, the more you make."

"Wow, I sure wish someone had explained that to me when I was a kid," Chuck joked. "I probably would have been a world-famous neurosurgeon by now."

"Was that what you wanted to be, a doctor?"

"Once upon a time, yeah. But a certain somebody put those dreams in the junkyard."

It was Susanna's turn to clear her throat at Chuck, but Ross saw an opportunity to find out where he stood. "Not to get too personal, but would that be the missing Mr. Kincaid?"

Ross looked at Kelly, but she just looked at her plate.

"That's right," Chuck answered flatly. "He ran out on us when I was eleven, and promptly crashed his plane. He's still alive as far as we know, but we've never seen or heard from him again, which is just fine with me."

"Chuck!" Susanna's voice was low, but filled with shame and dismay.

"It's okay, Mrs. Kincaid," Ross said. "I didn't mean to pry into your business, but I understand the way your son feels. Any man who would walk out on such a beautiful family is obviously a fool who doesn't deserve them."

Looking at the sadness in Susanna's and Kelly's eyes, and the anger in Chuck's, Ross could clearly see how much he'd been fooling himself about winning back their affections. They would never forgive him – why should they? And how could he stay in their lives as someone else? How long before they somehow found out, and hated him all the more?

Just then, the Nazarians showed up, with apologies for the car trouble that had delayed them.

"I know a really good mechanic," Chuck deadpanned to David's parents. "Oh, wait – he was in your car already!"

"It doesn't take a mechanic to change a flat tire in the driveway," David countered. "But it sure seems like a chore after you get used to having an air wrench."

"Mr. Morton, I'd like you to meet my family. This is my father, Aram, and my mother, Meghranoush."

"Isn't that a pretty name?" Kelly interjected. "It means 'sweet as honey.'"

"Thank you, Kelly," Mrs. Nazarian smiled. "But some people do find it hard to pronounce. You can just call me Meg," she added to Ross. "Almost everyone does, outside my family."

Ross shook her hand warmly. "And you can call me Ro..., uh, Roger. That goes for all of you, too – I hope we'll get to be very good friends." He sat back down, relieved that he'd stopped short of actually saying his real name, and that no one seemed to have noticed the slip.

"I also have three sisters," David continued, "but they are with my grandparents in Texas this week. By the way, Mr. Morton, did I mention that we lived near them for a while, in Arlington? Dad was actually in construction, so you probably know some of the same people."

Ross looked back at David's father, and suddenly, sickeningly, realized that he knew him. It was hard to forget a man who would turn down a six-figure drywall contract, just because the clinic they were building provided abortion services. So much for fate being on his side. What were the chances of running into him again twelve hundred miles away, and at the worst possible time?

"I was going to say," Aram remarked, "that you look very familiar, Mr. Morton, but I just can't place the name. Do you know...?"

The elder Nazarian began to list one after another of the men and companies that Ross had worked with for years. It was just a matter of time before he remembered. At the very least, he'd be curious enough to talk to his friends about it, and just like that, the ruse would be over. Suddenly the whole scheme looked to Ross like house of cards, built by an idiot – and the idiot was himself.

"Mr. Morton," Mrs. Nazarian interrupted with concern, "Are you all right?"

Actually, Ross was not all right – he felt as though the walls of the restaurant were closing in on him. He decided he'd better step outside and get some fresh air, and try to figure some way out of this fix. He mumbled an excuse and tried to rise from his chair, but was perplexed to find that his right arm wouldn't cooperate. It simply hung by his side, like a useless decoration.

"Mr. Morton, what's the matter?" Ross could read the alarm on Susanna's face.

Nothing, I'm fine, he tried to say, but he couldn't form the words. Instead of his voice, all that came out was a gravelly sort of moan. Half out of his chair, Ross's right leg crumpled beneath him. There were panicked voices, somebody was yelling to call 911 – but, surely this wasn't real.

For just a moment, he could see Jacob's face against a white hospital pillow case. *God has a locker with your name on it... eternal life... but you have to open it... He won't do that for you....*

And then, there was darkness.

26

Bills Past Due

Susanna had always hated hospital waiting rooms. They meant being close enough to the person she was worried about that she couldn't think of anything else, but at the same time, being too far away to be of any help. And it was in a hospital waiting room that Susanna and her father had received the news that her mother had died on the operating table, during emergency gall-bladder surgery.

What was a new experience for Susanna was having her church family there with her, and being able to pray. "It's not just the only thing we can do," Pastor Grayson reminded her, "it's the very best thing." And pray they did, with a fervency that was amazing, for a man most of them didn't even know.

Susanna herself found a strange urgency in her prayers. It wasn't just that Roger Morton didn't know the Lord, and might die tonight. It was as though there was a knowledge in her spirit that her mind wasn't privy to – that this man was somehow more to her than another soul in need of salvation. As though he was somehow her own special burden, and she had to see him through.

Mr. Morton hadn't regained consciousness since he collapsed in the restaurant. The emergency room doctors quickly diagnosed his condition as a massive stroke, brought on by prolonged hypertension, and probably stress factors as well. Thus far, no one had been able to find out who his next of kin might be, or who should be notified, as his condition was considered critical.

Father, Susanna silently prayed, *don't let this man enter into eternity without knowing you. Give us a chance to be a light to him, like you sent Tina to be a light to me.*

Susanna opened her eyes as a nurse touched her shoulder. "Mrs. Kincaid? I'm sorry to bother you, but the rest of your group seems to be asleep."

Susanna looked around at the faithful few, and confirmed the nurse's observation. "What time is it?" she asked the young woman.

"It's just after 3 AM," the nurse smiled. "I can't believe you're still awake. I wanted to let you know, though, that we believe your husband is out of danger."

Relief flooded Susanna's heart, and she quickly murmured a prayer of thanks. "He's not my husband, though," she corrected. "He's my son's new employer."

"Oh really?" the nurse looked confused. "I'm sorry, I guess I just assumed because of the name...."

"What name?" Now Susanna was confused. "His name is Roger Morton."

The nurse shuffled her paperwork and shook her head. "Somebody must have made a mistake. That's the name on the medical chart, but on the insurance paperwork, it says 'Ross Kincaid.'"

Susanna thought her heart must have stopped. It just couldn't be. It had to be some sort of mix-up, a crazy coincidence. But then again, it would explain so many things. And his face – he might have had plastic surgery, after the plane crash....

"Mrs. Kincaid, are you all right?"

Susanna tried to compose herself. "Uh, yes... that is... could you double check and see where they got that other name?"

The nurse readily agreed, and returned shortly with a very puzzled look. "It was on the health insurance card in his wallet," she explained. "But now it doesn't match his driver's license, so we can't figure out what's going on."

So it was true. Unbelievable, but true. It was Ross – trying to come back and make it up to them, after all these years. "I can explain, nurse," she said, with more calm than she felt. "But it might take a little while."

But explaining it to the doctors and nurses was one thing – explaining it to her children was another. She knew it would be easier with Kelly, so she started there, as they had breakfast in the hospital cafeteria a few hours later.

"I... I just... I can't believe it!" Kelly sputtered in obvious bewilderment. "It's like a crazy movie plot or something. What was he planning to do – try to marry you all over again?"

"I honestly don't know what he had in mind," Susanna admitted, "except that he must have thought he was making up for leaving us by helping Chuck.

I'm also suspicious that he may have tried to help me at the school board hearing. There were rumors that someone with a lot of money was working behind the scenes, and that's why Janet Osborne tried to quash the whole thing."

"You know, Mom," Kelly said, "I really thought I had forgiven Dad for what he did to us. But his coming in the back door like this just sort of makes me mad. Why couldn't he have just been honest, and said he was sorry?"

Susanna sighed heavily. "Facing up to your mistakes isn't easy, Kelly, especially without the Lord. I know: I ran from mine for as long as I could. But I've never stopped loving your dad. Since we met Jesus, I've been praying he would too – whether we ever saw him again or not. Now the Lord has given us a chance to show your dad what his forgiveness and love are like. I know that might be hard for you...."

"And impossible for Chuck," Kelly interjected. "Mom, he doesn't even know the Lord yet, and you know how bitter he is about Dad. He'll never take that job now, even if it's still available, and he'll hate Dad all the more for the disappointment."

"I know." Susanna sighed again. "But Kelly, the first thing we have do is settle things in our own hearts. We can't expect Chuck to let go of his bitterness and anger, if we hold on to any of our own."

Kelly sat for a while, reliving old memories – and letting them go. "I do forgive him, Mom," she finally said, with tears in her eyes. "I think I'd probably still have rebelled, even if he'd been there. But without him, I've had the chance to learn how much God wants to be my father. I want Dad to know Him too."

Together, mother and daughter bowed their heads, and prayed for the two men in their lives who needed the Lord: one, as he lay unconscious in his hospital room, and the other, as he was about to get the most shocking news of his life.

Susanna drove home to meet Chuck, who had gone there to shower and shave, planning to return afterward to the hospital. He met her in the kitchen, still brushing his damp, thick blond hair, and as he often did, he kissed her on the cheek. Ross used to do that every day, Susanna suddenly recalled, but he stopped when Chuck was still too young to remember. In some ways, he was so much like his dad.

"Sit down, Chuck," she said soberly. "There's something I have to tell you."

He grabbed a chair and sank down slowly, a look of dread on his face. "He's dead, isn't he?"

"No, Chuck, they say he's out of danger, but...."

Chuck immediately looked relieved. "But what, then? Why are you acting like the world just ended?"

Please Lord, let him understand, somehow. "Chuck," she began, "I don't know how to tell you this, but... Roger Morton is actually your father."

For a moment, he just stared at her in disbelief. Then, he began to laugh. "What is this, Mom – are we reenacting a scene from *Star Wars*? We'll I'm not Luke What's-His-Name, and Roger Morton is not my father! That's the most ridiculous thing...." He stopped, seeing her expression had not changed.

"I'm afraid it's true, Chuck. The hospital found his real name on an insurance card in his wallet. And when you think about it, it all makes sense...."

Chuck slammed his open palm into the tabletop, making Susanna jump. "No!" he shouted, his face growing dark with rage. "It does *not* make sense! Our deadbeat dad, who dumped us all like we were some sort of trash, suddenly shows up to be our fairy godfather? Whoever thinks that makes sense is crazy!"

"Chuck," his mom said gently, "please try to control yourself. I know this is a shock."

"Shock?" he repeated. "Oh no, this is just what I was expecting, Mom. Everything in my life goes this way! First I was going to be a doctor, but no, I couldn't do that because our wonderful, loving daddy walked out on us to marry his secretary, and I had to go to work. Forty-five hours a week in a two-bit garage, dreaming of the break I was going to get someday.

"Then, along comes that break, and how does it turn out? The same jerk who wrecked my first dream, wrecks the second one, too! That really figures. And you know, it's kind of funny, in a way. I guess the joke's on me!" He laughed a bitter, almost crazy laugh, but it began to sound more like a sob as he buried his face in his arms on the table.

Susanna was filled with pity for her son, and the helplessness she felt was like a painful ache in her heart. The only thing she had to offer, she knew he didn't want. Still, she sat down beside him, and put her arm around his broad shoulders.

"Chuck," she said softly, "I love you more than anything. You've stood beside me, and filled a man's shoes in this house long before you should have had to. I'm not denying that your father was responsible for that, although I have to take a share of the blame as well. And I'm not saying he chose the right way to come back to us. But Chuck, I've forgiven him, and so has Kelly – because Jesus forgave us."

Chuck jumped up angrily, pulling away from her embrace. "Mom, please! Don't bring God into this – not now! Where was Jesus when Dad walked out? Where was he when Kelly cried herself to sleep, and when the pain of the divorce drove you to drink? Where was he when I needed someone to teach me how to drive a car, or what to say to a girl, and all I had was my high school math teacher! Tell me, Mom, where was Jesus then?"

"He was right there, Chuck," Susanna replied tearfully. "He was standing outside our door, knocking – we just never heard Him."

"Yeah, well, he must have knocked pretty quietly, because I still don't hear him. All I hear is the sound of a world where everybody has it together but me, and I want my share. And I don't need a father who didn't think I was worth keeping ten years ago, coming back and doing me any favors. He can keep his stupid garage, and his millions of dollars, and that new face they pasted on him – he can take it all right back to Texas, and stay there, as far as I'm concerned!"

Susanna sighed, and looked at the floor.

"What is it?" Chuck demanded. "There's something else you're not telling me."

"I don't think it's the best time to discuss it, Chuck."

He sat back down, apparently spent from his outburst. "Might as well get it over with," he sighed.

Susanna ran a hand through her hair, tangled from the night she'd spent on the waiting room sofa. "Chuck, your father is facing a long recovery from this stroke, and he has no one to take care of him."

"So? He's got plenty of money – let him rent himself a sanatorium!" He stopped and looked at her. "Let me guess – you want to be his nurse?"

"The school year is almost over," Susanna explained, "and I have enough personal leave coming to cover what's left. I feel like the Lord wants me to invite your father to convalesce here – in his own room, of course."

Chuck didn't say anything for a long while. Finally, he got up with a shrug of his shoulders. "It's your house, Mom," he said flatly. "You can have anybody in it you want. But as long as that man is here, I won't be. I don't want to see him, or speak to him, ever again."

"Chuck, please...," Susanna attempted, but her son just walked out, leaving her sitting at the kitchen table.

27

Love The Stranger

When Ross first opened his eyes, everything was a blur. All around him was white, with just a few fuzzy splashes of color, here and there. As he turned his head, his eyes fixed on one particular patch of green. That particular shade had always been Susanna's favorite color – she had made him scour all the car lots halfway to the Mexican border, until he found a sedan in emerald green.

But Susanna's dead... she died in the plane crash. No... she isn't dead... she's back in California, and I'm.... Where am I?

Slowly, his memory began to return, and his eyes came into focus. The face above that patch of green wasn't Susanna's – and yet it looked so much like her, twenty years ago. *Kelly?* He tried to form the name, but his lips and tongue wouldn't work together, and the sound they made was strange, and hardly recognizable as his own voice.

The young woman, who had apparently been absorbed in a book, looked up immediately, and smiled. "Dad?"

Dad. Ross hadn't heard anyone call him that in nearly eleven years. It sounded odd, and almost wrong, like using someone else's identity. That thought brought back the memories of Roger Morton, and the dinner party... but after that was a blank.

"You've had a stroke," Kelly explained, apparently sensing his confusion, "and you've been out of it for a couple days. You're doing a lot better, but the doctor says you'll have a hard time talking, so don't worry about that for now."

She slipped her slim, soft hand into his thick, beefy one. "Squeeze my hand if you understand, okay?"

Ross squeezed, but he didn't understand. What was she doing here? She obviously knew who he really was: the father who had pushed her roughly away the last time she saw him, and left her alone when she needed him the most. And yet, she seemed genuinely happy to see him.

"I'm going to go phone Mom," she said, "and let the doctor know you've come around. I'll be right back."

As he watched his daughter leave the room, Ross had a strange thought. *What if she didn't come back? What if she went off, got married, and never spoke to me again? That's what I did to her, and Chuck... and Susanna. How will I ever face Susanna?*

Fortunately for Ross, he had no choice in the matter. Susanna, upon receiving Kelly's report, dropped what she was doing and drove straight to the hospital, praying all the way. *Lord, let your love flow through me.*

When she came in the room, Ross tried to sit up – a futile exercise in his current condition, with one side completely paralyzed. Susanna rushed the last few steps and made him lie back down again.

"Hello, Ross," she said. "I'm so glad to see you."

His lips moved, but she more read the question in his eyes, than heard it in his voice. "Why?"

"Because of Jesus," she replied simply.

Ever so slightly, he seemed to shake his head. Could he ever believe it? Was it too simple, too childish for that proud, determined, active mind?

"Ross," she said, "the doctors tell us that you're going to need a lot of rest and care. We've already been in touch with your business partners, and they know not to expect to hear from you for at least a few months. I want you to come home with us for the summer."

There, again, was that slight shake of the head. Susanna decided to ignore it for the moment.

"I know it might seem a little strange, and you will find that a lot of things have changed. But Ross, the most important thing that's happened since you left, happened just a few months ago. Kelly and I both met Jesus, and He has completely transformed our lives.

"I guess you thought you needed to come under a different name so we would accept you, but believe me, Ross, it wasn't necessary. Once I found out how great God's grace really is, I couldn't hold on to any bitterness or anger anymore. I forgive you, Ross, completely and unconditionally."

The look in his eyes was still one of disbelief. Slowly, he turned toward Kelly. "I forgive you too, Dad," she said simply. "Mom and I want to take care of you, and I hope you'll let us do it."

Susanna saw something then that she hadn't seen before, not in all the years she'd known Ross, from the first day they met. A small tear formed in his eye, and rolled down his cheek onto the pillow. He nodded, and again tried to speak. Susanna couldn't be sure, but she thought he was trying to say "thank you."

It was, at least, a sign of hope. Doubtless Ross had his own reasons for coming back to them, but Susanna felt sure that it was God who was really behind it. Old wounds might have to be reopened before they could heal, but she had no doubt that healing was the end He had in mind.

"I'm sure you noticed that Chuck's not here, Ross," Susanna said carefully. "Unfortunately, he didn't have the same experience as Kelly and I did, and I'm afraid he hasn't forgiven you. In fact, he's moving out of the house, and he won't be coming to see us as long as you're there." He nodded, looking sad, Susanna thought, but not surprised. Chuck's attitude was probably a lot easier for him to understand and accept, than unconditional forgiveness.

"Oh, and by the way," Kelly added as she remembered, "the man who was going to sell you his garage backed out when he found out you had a double identity. I guess he thought you must be a mafia boss or something."

Susanna thought she could detect a hint of a smile at the corner of Ross's mouth. She wondered if he still remembered how funny he used to find their little girl's bluntness. "At least her husband will never have to wonder what she's thinking!" he had laughed.

Those were the sort of memories she'd tried to suppress over the years, when she couldn't stand the pain. How did he feel about them now? Was he sorry for all the things he'd missed?

Questions such as these were to remain unanswered, at least for the first few weeks of Ross's recovery. Beyond meaningful looks, and a few short sentences, he couldn't tell anyone what he was thinking if he had wanted to. The only thing that was clear about Ross to his family, and everyone else that encountered him, was that he didn't intend to let the stroke beat him. His physical and speech therapists said he worked harder than any patient they'd ever known, as though he really had something to live for. Just what that something was, for the moment, only he knew.

Susanna and Kelly both did their best to minister to Ross, without taking advantage of the fact that he was a captive audience. Kelly offered to read to her dad from the Bible one afternoon, and was surprised when he not only agreed, but asked her to continue when she tried to stop. Susanna knew better than to read too much into that, though. Ross had always been curious about everything, and probably his main interest in the Scripture was finding out what made his ex-wife and daughter tick.

As Ross regained his strength, Susanna began bringing him up the street to the clubhouse in a wheelchair. He seemed to enjoy the company of the children, and especially watching Kelly work and play with them. The Jesus Gang had finally gotten off the ground, thanks to a generous personal gift from a most unexpected source: Judge Lisa Rohrman of the juvenile court. She was quite surprised when the "arsonists" actually completed their community service, and didn't quickly reappear in her courtroom on other charges, as was so often the case. Concluding that this "gang" was actually one of the more effective rehabilitation programs in town, she decided to get behind the work, and convinced several of her friends to do the same.

The clubhouse, decorated in such riotous colors as appealed to the rather outlandish tastes of its denizens, quickly became a focal point for the neighborhood. Since the members of the club were pledged to strict secrecy, the goings-on inside the little house soon became a matter of great curiosity to the uninitiated. Eventually, even a few of the older kids risked the embarrassment of being seen to darken the door of "that Jesus house," as the place had become known.

The first evening that a group of these teenagers showed up, Kelly nearly panicked. Mr. Pillow had stopped coming to every meeting once the community service was done, and it became clear that the club members weren't really any kind of threat. Leaving an almost equally intimidated Beth in charge, Kelly ran to the nearest house that had a phone, and called in reinforcements. A short time later, her cavalry arrived in the form of David Nazarian.

Although David had taken his old job back when Ross's deal fell through, he had confided to Kelly that he felt the Lord was calling him into full-time ministry. Just what kind of ministry, he wasn't sure, but he felt that working with the neighborhood kids was as good a place as any to start. At first, he just "hung out" with the teens, playing basketball, and listening to their problems. Eventually, he was able to interest a few in learning the basics of auto repair, which was considerably more constructive than some of their former pastimes.

When Kelly and David were at the clubhouse together, it was fairly easy to imagine them as a family, with all their young "gangsters" as their adopted children. No one was going to rush into anything, though. David had shared with Kelly that he had prayed about their relationship, and received a one-word answer: "Wait." That was okay with both Kelly and Susanna, as experience was already teaching them that it was best to trust the Lord, and let Him open the doors they needed to walk through.

A much greater temptation to worry presented itself to Susanna in the form of her increasingly wayward son. Unlike David, he had refused to go back to Rocky Philips, and had launched precipitously into business for himself instead. The only garage he could afford to rent was in a part of town where no one wanted to be at night, a fact to which the bars on every business door and window mutely attested.

He had managed to bring enough customers with him to make ends meet – just barely, as far as anyone could tell. Susanna and Kelly visited him as often as they could, although he had so far kept his promise not to set foot in the house where his father was a guest. Realizing that his little game of dabbling in religion was over, he had dropped that particular pretense, and left his "OPEN" sign up seven days a week.

Chuck wasn't quite ready to give up on his relationship with Beth, though, finding it had outgrown the "score a few dates" goal he'd originally set. Hoping she might feel the same way, he arranged an "accidental" meeting on her college campus during a study period one afternoon.

"Hello there, bookworm," he said as he plopped on the grass beside her. "Figured out how to solve all the world's problems yet?"

"Oh, someone else already figured that one out," she smiled in reply, "and even put it in a bestselling book. But I think you've heard that story."

"Several times," he nodded. "And I'm not saying I don't believe it. Certainly seems to work for some people."

"But not you?"

"You know, Beth," he sighed, "I really wish we could have at least one conversation that doesn't take a turn down the sawdust trail in the first two minutes. There are other things in life besides faith, you know."

"I'm afraid there aren't in my life," she said frankly. "At least, not anything that matters. Jesus *is* my life, Chuck – without Him, I'm not anything."

"I beg to differ," Chuck objected. "You're a sweet, lively, intelligent girl, and if God made you that way, I'm sure He wants you to enjoy your life, and not spend it all moping about religion."

"Of course God wants us to be happy, Chuck," Beth replied earnestly, "but not just for the moment. Happiness that comes from money, success, and romance is like the good feeling you get from drugs, or drink: it all goes away by morning and leaves you with an awful headache. The happiness Jesus gives starts on the inside, and just keeps growing and growing. Best of all, it won't end when we die – we'll be with Him forever."

"Hey, if there is a Heaven, I want to go," Chuck insisted. "And I may be convinced one day. But I think I've got a few years left to think about it, and right now, I have better things to do."

"I wouldn't take that chance if I were you," Beth advised. "What if you had to stand before God tonight – what would you say?"

"Well, I guess I'd have to apologize for doubting his existence, for starters," Chuck snickered. "But you guys are always talking about how God is merciful and forgiving – I don't see why he wouldn't let me in. It's not like I've killed anyone or anything."

"Jesus said that hatred is the same as murder," Beth said quietly. "And He is forgiving, but He also made it clear that if we don't forgive, we can't be forgiven."

Chuck's smile disappeared. "If you're going to get on me about forgiving my dad, Beth, you can forget it. If that's what it takes to get into Heaven, God can count me out. Some things just aren't forgivable, and what he did is one of them."

"I just wish you could see, Chuck," Beth attempted, "how much your bitterness against your dad is hurting *you*. Holding a grudge is like drinking poison and hoping the other person dies."

"Oh, I don't want him to die," Chuck replied with a note of sarcasm. "I want him around to see what I can do without him. But I'm sure you've never harbored a moment's resentment of your parents for what they did to you. Oh, wait! You were raised in a loving home with great parents. Sorry, my bad!"

Beth tried to answer as Chuck got up and dusted himself off, but he wasn't listening.

"I don't need any of you," he declared. "Not you, or your Jesus, or my dad, or anyone else. I can get along all by myself. I'll show you all – just wait and see."

The tears began to roll down Beth's cheeks as she watched him stride angrily across the campus, growing smaller and smaller until she could see him no more.

"Father," she prayed, "I didn't mean to care for Chuck, but you know I do. Now I have to leave him in your hands. I'm not asking for you to bring him back to me, but whatever it takes – please bring him back to You."

28

Too Much Light

Almost breathless with exertion, but feeling an elating sense of accomplishment, Ross sat down heavily in the chair where he spent most of his days. He had just crossed the room, and returned, with only the aid of a cane. Time was when he'd have taken less satisfaction in building an entire apartment complex, but now that seemed almost like a different life. The stroke, and the last three months he'd spent in the care and company of his family, had given him a new perspective on a lot of things.

The communication barrier had been frustrating at times, yet strangely enlightening, too. Like his secret identity, his disability had also been a kind of two-way mirror, letting him see people as they truly were – himself included.

Most of his adult life, Ross had been a "mover and shaker." The people around him had paid attention to what he said, gauged his reactions, and tried to impress him with their intelligence. But Ross Kincaid in a wheelchair, who couldn't even form a simple sentence without herculean effort – hardly anyone paid attention to him. They were busy getting on with their lives, just as he had been a few months before.

If anyone did speak to him, out of obligation or kindness, they would usually betray a perfectly understandable misapprehension: if someone can't talk very well, there must be something wrong with his mind. And so they would say the silliest things, in a slow, loud voice that they might use with a child or a deaf, senile old man. Sometimes, Ross couldn't keep himself from laughing, which probably just added to their impression that he wasn't right in his head.

Ross had worked very hard – harder than he ever had in his life, in fact – to get his speech and mobility back. But when the situation called for it, he wasn't above pretending that he couldn't find the words, when he really just didn't want to answer the question. If Susanna and Kelly were wise to his tricks, they never let on, but just kept patiently waiting on him – in every sense of the word. The forgiveness and self-sacrifice they had shown, for a man they both should have hated, was the most amazing thing Ross had ever witnessed. It was the strongest evidence he had yet seen that Jesus was real.

Ross knew that what his wife and daughter wanted, more than anything in the world, was for him to become a Christian. But that was one thing he had determined never to lie to them about. The day he made up his mind to follow God, he would go all the way. But the truth was, he just wasn't ready to go there right now. To profess faith in Christ, as a broken man who could barely walk and talk, just didn't sit well with his pride. It was like finally admitting he needed the crutch after all, and that, he couldn't force himself to do.

What he had come to terms with, over the last few months, was the truth of the wretched, self-centered life he had lived. He realized now how much he had deserved every moment of unhappiness that ever came his way, just as he *didn't* deserve the kindness he was now experiencing at the hands of those he had betrayed.

And yet, Ross still held out hope that he might one day earn the love that was already his for the taking. That he could walk down the aisle with Susanna again, say "until death do us part," and prove that he could mean it this time. That when he gave his life to God, he'd be laying down something worth having, and not just the wreckage of a life given over to blind ambition.

Of course, Ross never shared any of this with Susanna or Kelly, even when his recovery finally made that possible. He knew the sorts of things they'd say, but this was between him and his conscience: a battle he had to fight, to prove himself worthy of being forgiven. All he would tell them was that he was "on the road" to believing, and they didn't press him further. He knew they were praying, and though that fact would have once bothered him, he now found it comforting.

"Susanna," he said when she came in the room. "Been thinking. Summer's over, and... need to get out of your house. Shouldn't be keeping you from... Chuck." How he hated the choppy way those sentences came out. But she just smiled, as she always did, and sat down beside him.

"Ross, you know you're welcome to stay here for as long as you want. You can be at home alone now, and as for Chuck, we see him often enough at his apartment, and other places."

"I know," he insisted, "but it's... I'm... in your way. I need to go back... home for a while. Take care of some things."

Susanna looked puzzled, probably wondering what could possibly be in Texas that would make it "home" to him. "I don't see how you can make it without help," she said. "And both Kelly and I would be really sorry to see you go."

"I'll be back," he insisted, "probably... next spring. And... find help too. Not like you, though." He said the last part with a tender smile, and touched Susanna's hand. It reminded her of the old days – but she knew she couldn't go back there. For her to have a relationship with Ross again, a right foundation had to be laid first. Otherwise, it would fall apart one day, the same as it had before.

"Well," she sighed, "if that's what you feel like you need to do, just tell me when, and what we can do to help."

Kelly went to her room soon after receiving the news that Ross was leaving, and secretly cried. It wasn't like the last time, of course – he was more dependent on them than the other way around. But she had pinned a lot of her hopes on the idea that her father and brother would get saved, and they could be a family again.

"Kelly," Susanna counseled her later, "we have to give your dad room to make his own choices. I don't think he's making the right one either, but until he turns his life over to the Lord, that's to be expected. God won't have any trouble finding him in Texas, any more than right here in our house."

Having planned his departure for a Sunday, Ross agreed to attend a final church service with Susanna and Kelly. Ross hadn't been in many churches in his life, but he had seen enough to know that this one broke all the stereotypes. Not only did they meet in an auto parts store, they had no pulpit, and didn't take up a collection. The worship, thanksgiving, and even the preaching all had an unvarnished, spontaneous quality that Ross found fascinating.

Pastor Grayson Farmer might have lacked the rhetorical polish of a seminarian, but he never seemed to care what sort of a personal impression he made anyway. Since this Sunday's sermon was the last he'd be hearing (at least for quite a while) Ross had decided to pay closer attention to the message, which was on the theme of "walking in the light." As he quite often did, Pastor Grayson invoked a real-life example from his former career.

"I tried to sell some more efficient, brighter lighting to a factory one time," he said. "But even though we could show how the upgrade would pay for itself within a few years, someone on the maintenance team kept stonewalling us. After a few months of going around in circles, I finally managed to find out who it was: the safety supervisor! It turned out that he was afraid more light would let the OSHA inspectors see things on the manufacturing floor that weren't up to code.

"Now isn't that ironic? This guy, whose job it was to improve safety at the plant, rejected the one thing they needed most: the light to see the problems. And yet, he really wasn't that different from most of us. We say we want to change, but we want to do it ourselves, in the dark, where no one can see. Friends, let me assure you that God doesn't work that way. On day one of Creation, the first thing He did was to turn the lights on. I guarantee that until you are willing to let Him do that in your life, you'll only change to become more and more like yourself."

Susanna wasn't one to say "amen" out loud in church, but her heart was shouting out an agreement with the message that she hoped the man sitting beside her could somehow hear. Having experienced the freedom that came through opening up all the doors and windows of her own heart, she longed for both Ross and Chuck to do the same.

But if Ross was impacted by the sermon, he didn't show it. As he boarded the plane that afternoon, he had that same determined look she had seen in his face the day he left her for Colleen. "I'll be back," he reminded her, as if reading her thoughts. "This time... I promise... things will be different."

29

Self Improvement

A groan of strain escaped Ross's lips as he gave one more pull on the weights, then let them thump to the bottom of the machine.

"Very good, Mr. Kincaid!" effused his physical therapist. She'd have said the same thing, Ross knew, if he hadn't moved the weights an inch. It was after 5 P.M., and she wanted to go home.

"It wasn't good at all," he grumbled, mopping his face with a towel. "I did better yesterday."

"You're too hard on yourself," she consoled. "Why, you've made more progress in the last five months than some of my patients have in years!"

Ross merely grunted at the compliment. It was true that his limitations weren't anything like what they'd once been. Except for the limp in his gait, and the occasional pause in a sentence when the right word eluded him, one would hardly know he'd ever had a stroke.

But the only result that would completely satisfy Ross was to be back to the shape he was in a year ago – if only his recalcitrant brain and muscles would cooperate. He wouldn't go back to his family until he could do it without feeling like a burden – and going back was almost the only thing he ever thought about these days.

After ten years of a hermit-like, work-centered existence, Ross was no stranger to loneliness. But having spent the last summer in an atmosphere of real love and real life, he had found it very hard to readjust to his empty apartment, and the courteous, but disengaged company of his hired nurse.

Although he was able to go back to work part time, it was only because he owned a majority stake in the company that his rather inefficient efforts were tolerated. Everyone around him seemed to assume that his days as a major player in the construction business were finished. Sometimes, Ross was tempted to give up and admit they were right. But then, he'd look at the picture of Susanna and Kelly on his bedside table, and resolve once again to prove he could be the man he once was – only better.

Letters from "home" (as he now thought of Susanna's house) were the high points of his week. Kelly was doing much better academically in her senior year, and hoped to graduate with at least a B average. David had gone on a short-term mission to Armenia, his ancestral homeland, but was staying in touch with a long letter to Kelly about every other day. His last letter had contained a tantalizing bit about something important he would share in person, when he came home in a few weeks.

Chuck's business seemed to be prospering, though from the tone of Susanna's letters, one might have thought the opposite was the case. One thing Ross never could grasp about Susanna and her church was their apparent distaste for success. Although the grudge Chuck bore against him still bothered Ross, he was also proud of his son, in a way. *I guess it's just as well that I didn't wind up helping him*, he thought. *This way, he'll learn to make it on his own. Maybe, someday, we'll find a way to patch things up between us.*

One evening when he checked his mailbox, Ross was surprised to find a personal letter there that didn't bear Susanna's return address. It was from Hannah Wertheim, of all people. Ross had almost forgotten he had left her his address, along with his offer of help, which she was now apparently going to accept.

Dear Mr. Kincaid,

First of all, I want to thank you again for your kindness in bringing us Jacob's last letter. I am so sorry that you didn't receive a warmer welcome at our house, but please understand that the news you brought was a very great shock. I hope you will not consider it too great an imposition if I ask you now for another favor.

You may or may not be aware that, in his youth, Jacob was involved with a troubled young woman, who became pregnant as a result of the relationship. Since the girl was not Jewish, Jacob couldn't marry her, but we gave her some money, and encouraged her to put the child up for adoption, rather than aborting it. We later learned that she did neither: the child was born healthy, and her mother named her Kristen. She would be fourteen years old in March.

After his conversion to Christianity several years later, Jacob became very interested in locating his daughter, so that he could at least help to provide for her needs. In this he was not successful, but he kept a special bank account where he put aside all the money he could spare, to be used for Kristen if and when she could be found. He asked us to continue this search, as we were able.

My husband, as you may imagine, has little interest in honoring Jacob's request, but he will not interfere with my efforts to do so. Having exhausted all the options that have occurred to an old woman, I write to you in the hopes that you might have learned something from your conversations with Jacob, or found something in his Bible, that might be relevant.

All we know of the little girl's mother is that her name was Sara Gonzales, and her last known address was in San Diego. We understand she has been married at least once, so it's quite likely she has a different name by now, and perhaps has given it to her daughter as well. Her family has not heard from her in over twelve years, and regrettably, they don't seem to care much at all.

Mr. Kincaid, that little girl is all that is left in this world of my son Jacob. If there is

anything you can do to help me find her, I beg
you, please do it.

Yours Sincerely,

Hannah Wertheim

Ross put the letter down, took off his reading glasses, and smiled. Limp or no limp, he couldn't pass up this chance to help someone, finally, in a real way. It was time to make another trip back home, and look up an old acquaintance.

30
Kristen

"I hope you realize I don't do taxi service for just anybody," Phil complained through the open passenger door. "Especially not when it means coming to a crowded airport."

"Yeah, nice to see you too, Phil," Ross quipped, climbing with some difficulty into the private eye's inexpressibly dirty jeep. "But if you're gonna call this... this rolling clod a taxi, I think you'd better take it to a car wash first."

Phil shook his head as though Ross had just said something ridiculous. "Tell me, Mr. K., if you were looking for a car to steal, would you pick this one?"

"Are you kidding? You couldn't pay any self-respecting thief to heist this thing."

"Exactly," Phil nodded sagely, as though the superiority of his logic was self-evident.

"Never mind," Ross sighed, "I didn't come here to... debate the merits of automobile hygiene. You said in your message that you found Kristen Gonzales?"

"Kristen Marsh," Phil corrected. "Her mom married a deadbeat named Reggie Marsh about nine years ago, and stayed hitched just long enough to make her hubby's last name stick to the kid. That's what made it so hard to find her."

"So where is she?" Ross pressed. "Still with her mom?"

"Sure hope not. Sara Gonzales has been a guest of the State of California for the last five years, and will be for another ten to twenty. 'Persistent offender,' is the term the judge used. In her case, it's just another word for a hopeless drug addict. Can't figure out what to do with 'em, so we just lock 'em up and throw the key away."

"So what became of her daughter?" Ross had no patience today for the detective's customary digressions.

"Dumped into the foster care system," Phil shrugged, "like about a half a million others. Too many kids, too few case workers, not enough good homes – it's a real mess."

"Are you saying she's in a bad situation?" Ross asked apprehensively.

"You could say that. Her current foster mom looks pretty good on paper: you have to, or they won't let you into the system. Trouble is her boyfriends – and boy, can she pick 'em. The creep who's living there now hasn't been busted lately, but he's overdue. Been into drugs, armed robbery, the works. Certifiable head case, too."

Ross was aghast. "So what do we do to get her out of there – report them to Social Services?"

"Sure," Phil snorted, "if you want to get wrapped from head to toe in red tape and stuffed in a filing cabinet in some bureaucrat's office."

"Yeah, that's just what I had in mind," Ross retorted. "If the system is that broken, what options *do* we have?"

"Well, first things first, we get rid of Mr. Bad-news Boyfriend for a while. Then at least you can talk to the foster mom, and see if the girl's all right."

Without waiting for his plan to be approved, Phil pulled over, picked up his car phone, and dialed, carefully disguising his voice when he spoke.

"Yeah, I'd like to report some drug-related activity at 839 West Campanella Street. Yeah, the parties over there are as high as Pike's Peak. Seems like they've got a kid in the house, too. Yeah... uh-huh. Thanks very much."

He hung up, a sly grin on his face, and switched on his police radio. Within a few moments, the dispatcher was relaying Phil's report to a cruiser in the area. "Happen to know this guy's got a police scanner too," he explained. "So the coast should be clear by the time we get there."

It had been quite a while since Ross had visited the part of San Diego that Phil was headed into now. Each street looked seedier than the last, lined with dilapidated houses that looked like they were just waiting for a wrecking ball to come and put them out of their misery. He thought about how easily Kelly could have ended up in the sort of situation Kristen was in now, stuck in a system that was too small to help, and too big to care. Inwardly, he shuddered at the complacence he'd shown over the last ten years. At least Jacob had cared enough to try and find his daughter.

Staring out the window at the dismal passing scenery, Ross caught a glimpse of a teenage girl, trudging down the alley toward a bus stop. Her backpack looked overloaded, as though it might contain more than just schoolbooks. It was too late for her to be coming home from school, anyway. And the face... surely it couldn't be.

"Phil," Ross said suddenly, "I'm going to play a hunch. Go around the block and let me off near that bus stop back there."

"I know you don't think much of my car, Mr. K.," Phil replied seriously, "but the bus won't take you where we're going. Anyway, it's only about six blocks from here."

"Yeah, I know, but I've got a feeling we might have just passed the girl we're looking for. Now I'm paying you by the hour, so will you just do like I say?"

Shaking his head and muttering darkly, Phil made an unnecessarily sharp turn, and pulled over about twenty yards from the bus stop where the girl was now sitting. Ross climbed out and walked toward her, leaning on his cane a little more than he needed to, so she wouldn't feel threatened.

"Mind if I sit down?" Ross managed a smile as he asked the question, but he was genuinely quite winded. The girl looked up, and just barely returned his smile as she moved over to make room on the bench. Her pale face had a look of almost permanent sadness, Ross thought. And those dark eyes – so much like Jacob's. Maybe he was crazy, or maybe Somebody had just whispered it in his ear, but he was sure enough now to take a chance.

"Are you Kristen Marsh?" he asked quietly.

The girl almost jumped, and shot a fearful glance in his direction. "I don't know what you're talking about," she said, and turned away, blushing. Ross almost laughed. He had met some bad liars in his time, but this girl was hopeless. The problem now was getting her to trust him.

"Listen," he said carefully, "I know this is going to sound weird, but you need to hear me out. I'm not a cop – you can leave any time you like, and obviously..." (he gestured toward his cane) "I can't stop you."

She scooted just an inch or two further away, but turned back toward him with a look of careful assessment. "Who are you?"

"My name is Ross Kincaid, and I knew your dad. I know that probably doesn't mean anything to you, because you never met him, but he searched for you for years. I'm sorry to say that he passed away without ever being able to find out what happened to you." He paused, wondering how that piece of news would affect her, but her expression remained unchanged.

"I've also met your grandparents – their names are Henry and Hannah Wertheim. Your grandmother took up the search after your dad passed on, and asked me to help. I know about your foster mom and her boyfriend. Is he the reason you're running away?"

She got up tensely, and leaned against the side of the shelter, apparently contemplating flight.

"I don't blame you at all," Ross added quickly. "From the little I know about that situation, it sounds like you've got good reason. I'd like to help you, but I can't, unless you let me."

She gave him another long, searching look, and finally sat back down with a sigh. "I guess it doesn't make much difference," she said. "I'll probably get picked up and sent back sooner or later, anyway."

"Not if I can help it," Ross said firmly. "But you need to tell me everything you can. Were you hurt there?"

She shook her head, fighting tears. "Just scared," she said. "Sadie is okay, but her boyfriend.... He's a dope pusher, and a thief, and he's... crazy. One minute he acts real nice, and the next minute he starts screaming that he's going to kill both of us, and himself too.

"The police showed up today, but he wouldn't let Sadie answer the door. They finally gave up and left, and he started yelling about how we'd turned him in, and broken his radio so he wouldn't know the cops were coming. I just hid in my room while they argued; she told him to get out, and he said he wouldn't, so she finally left. She just left me there with him." She repeated the words, as if still unable to believe it had happened.

"So you just slipped out the back?" Ross guessed.

Kristen nodded. "He was sitting on the couch drinking when I left. I don't think he really cared if I stayed or not, but I just couldn't. Maybe in a few days, he'll move on, and I can go back."

"Absolutely not," Ross declared, feeling a paternal instinct that he hadn't known in years. "That woman is obviously unfit to take care of you. You can stay with... my family for a while, until we can work something out."

"Thank you," she said quietly, and then started to cry. Ross laid his hand awkwardly on her shoulder. "Everything's going to... be okay," he promised. "We're going to find you a real family."

Ross waved at Phil to bring his car up, but Phil obviously didn't like the situation, and very distinctly shook his head. Ross pulled the folded *L.A. Times* out of his coat pocket, and wagged it with a meaningful look, which got his point across, and the Jeep in gear.

Money might cut it with Phil, but with a sobbing, fourteen-year-old runaway now in his care, Ross was glad he knew where to find something even more powerful: love.

31
Valentine's Day

Sometimes Susanna found it hard to believe that only about a year had passed since she met her Savior. The memory of her existence before that indelible demarcation now seemed like a black-and-white *film noir* from the forties, with no ending and no point. The past year, by contrast, had been filled with such color and surprise, such *life*, that it seemed more like a decade.

Things in the Kincaid house had already been bustling, with preparations for a baby shower for Tina (who was expecting her fifth child) and a homecoming party for David. Then came the totally unexpected phone call from Ross, with the news that he was not only back in town, he was bringing a teenage runaway over for Susanna to take care of!

The extra guest wasn't a problem, of course. The spare bedroom was unoccupied at the moment, although these days it seemed that there was someone staying there more often than not. But there were a few legal issues to consider, and the first number Susanna dialed, after hanging up the phone with Ross, was that of their friend, Judge Rohrman.

"Sometimes the system just doesn't work the way it's supposed to," the judge sighed when she'd heard the story. "Technically, what Ross did could be considered interference with custody, but I don't think anyone's going to press charges. There's certainly no law against your giving a homeless girl a place to stay. In the meantime, I'll set things in motion to get Kristen formally removed from that woman's house."

"But what happens after that?" Susanna asked. "Will she just go back into the system again?"

"Probably," the judge conceded, "unless her grandparents are willing to take her in. But not all foster homes are bad. I know some really good Christian foster parents. The only trouble is, none of them are ready to take in a teenager on short notice."

"Just hypothetically," asked Susanna on impulse, "what does it take to become a foster parent?"

The answer to that casual inquiry, which arrived the next day in the form of five thick folders of paperwork, almost made Susanna faint. She had heard of cutting down forests to fuel bureaucracy, but this was ridiculous. And with all the work she already had to do, the idea seemed impossible. So, she turned her attention for the moment to a soul that needed help: the kind of help that, thankfully, you didn't need a state license to dispense.

Kristen was a very sweet girl, and took to Susanna and Kelly right away. Never having known what it was to have a normal family, she seemed almost overwhelmed by the love that was immediately showered on her, not only by her hosts, but by their whole church as well. It was quickly discovered that Kristen had an unusual gift: babies placed in her arms, no matter how fussy, would quickly quiet down and go to sleep. This unique ability soon made the girl much in demand as a babysitter, and she loved every minute of it.

Ross found himself just slightly envious at not being noticed quite as much this time around. Susanna and Kelly were obviously glad to see him, though, and properly impressed with the physical progress he'd made. It was also nice, for once, to be able to stand back and take satisfaction in having made someone else's life better.

Having been the bearer of such awful news to Hannah Wertheim previously, Ross particularly enjoyed the duty of calling to tell her that Kristen had been found. The occasion was one of joy for her, of course, but it was marred somewhat by the continued stubbornness of her husband, who refused to have anything to do with his granddaughter. Mindful of his own years of hardness, Ross wished he could somehow make the old man understand what he was shutting himself out of.

Regardless of her husband's attitude, however, Hannah didn't intend to repeat the mistake she had made with her son. She got on a bus and showed up one afternoon on Susanna's doorstep, suitcase in hand. After introducing herself to Kelly, who answered the door, she hastened to explain that she wasn't looking for a place to stay.

"I'll be going on to a hotel this evening," she said. "But when I saw that the bus was going right through your neighborhood, I just had to get off. I couldn't wait one more minute to see my granddaughter."

This was a request that Susana and Kelly were happy to fulfill. Since they were rearranging furniture that afternoon, the living room was unavailable, so Hannah was invited to sit at the same kitchen table that had seen the breakup of the Kincaid family so many years ago. That it should now be the scene of a long-delayed but divinely ordained reunion, was just another one of the sweet ironies of grace.

"Kristen?" The old woman got up as her grandchild entered shyly. She drew close, and took the girl's face in her hands.

"You have your father's eyes, *meydele*," she said, her voice trembling. "Eyes I never thought to see again in this world. Bless God for his mercy!" She wrapped her arms around Kristen, and they cried together. Their hosts quietly withdrew to give the two of them some time alone, singing silent praises to the Father who can mend what his children have broken.

Needless to say, perhaps, Hannah Wertheim didn't go to a hotel that evening, nor any night for the following week of her visit. She and Kristen spent much of the time together, with Hannah telling her granddaughter stories of what her father was like: how smart he was, how studious, and what promise he had shown as a jeweler. Of course, such stories inevitably led to hard questions, for which Hannah had no answer that Kristen would understand.

"But why did he have to leave?" she wanted to know. "Was it so awful that he decided to be a Christian? The Kincaids are Christians, and they're wonderful people!"

"Yes, I know, child," she tried to explain, "but they were not born Jews. Tradition is everything to our people – it's what has kept us alive through centuries of hatred and persecution. I still didn't want your father to go, but I let your grandfather convince me it was best. He was sure that Jacob would come back to our faith eventually – that he would never be happy separated from us and our people. But in a way, I think he was, though it also made him very sad. It was we who were truly unhappy."

"But, I'm half Jewish, right?" Kristen asked. "Does that mean I can't be a Christian?'"

Hannah shook her head. "*Meydele*, you can be anything you want to be. I will always love you, no matter what. Jew or Christian, I believe that God loves each of us, and made us to love each other."

"That's right!" Kristen exclaimed. "It was in the little book Kelly gave me. It said that God loved us all so much, He gave his Son to die for us! But...." she hesitated. "Is that in your half of the Bible, or theirs?"

Her grandmother smiled. "Some say both, little one. But we shall have to read it together, to find out for sure."

And read it they did, using Jacob's Bible, which Ross had given Kristen. Hannah had many questions, some of which called for more knowledgeable answers from Don Pillow or Pastor Grayson.

Like Ross, Hannah was surprised to learn that Jesus and the apostles were all Jews. She learned for the first time, also, that the Nazis were not Christians. She heard the stories of many real Christians, even those who called themselves Lutherans, who helped the Jews during the Holocaust, sometimes ending up in the death camps along with them. The more both Hannah and Kristen discovered about this man named Jesus, and his true followers, the more they both seemed inclined to follow Him too.

The last day of Mrs. Wertheim's visit happened to be the same as David's homecoming party, which also coincided (by no one's particular design) with Valentine's Day. Now, as a rule, Kelly didn't allow herself to be preoccupied with romantic notions. David had said the Lord had told him to wait, and that was that. But she never could see herself with anyone else, and the hint he'd dropped about an important announcement, combined with the overtones of the day... well, it was hard not to jump to conclusions.

So, when David rose at the end of the party and asked for everyone's attention, Kelly felt her heart begin to beat faster with both excitement and trepidation.

"As I told some of you in my letters," David began, "the Lord revealed something very important to me on my trip, something that I'd like to share with you all now. With the blessing of my parents, I'm making plans to answer God's call, and become a missionary to the people of Armenia."

Kelly felt her heart sink through the floor. A missionary was just what she wanted to be, too – but now he would be going without her. Probably he'd meet some far more spiritual young woman over there, and that would be the end of it. She tried to put her own feelings aside, and offer joyful encouragement like everyone else was doing, but she knew it wasn't going to work. She just had to go someplace alone and cry.

"Wait a minute, Kelly!" David called as he saw her leaving. "I haven't passed out the presents yet. Here, Mr. Kincaid, would you give this one to Kelly?"

Ross passed her a large, but very light box, and Kelly tried to look interested as she opened it.

"I hope you like it," David said with a smile.

Must be a hat or something, Kelly thought as she undid the wrapping, and pulled out a layer of crumpled tissue paper. But no, there was another, smaller box inside. And another inside that. *What in the world...?*

Kelly hadn't noticed that the room had suddenly grown quiet as she pulled out the last box, a very small one that fit in the palm of her hand.

"I guess they over-packaged it a little," David chuckled, moving over to where she sat. "Here, let me help you with that last one."

He took the box, opened it, and produced a small, but beautiful diamond ring. Going down on one knee, he held it before her.

"Kelly," he said tenderly, "I thought of you every single day I was away. I prayed, and prayed, because I had to be sure it was the Lord. I knew He was sending me to Armenia, but I didn't know if I was supposed to just go alone. Then one day He said to me, 'I sent my disciples out two by two.' I've asked for, and received permission from your family, so now I'm asking you – will you be my wife?"

Kelly glanced at her mom, who looked incredibly happy and sad all at once, and at her dad, who just smiled, with a wistful look in his eyes. She only wished Chuck would have been here to share this moment with her.

"Yes!" she almost screamed, flinging her arms around David and nearly knocking him to the floor. There was a flurry of hugs, handshakes, tears and congratulations all around.

"I expect you to take care of my little girl, young man," Susanna admonished. "Armenia isn't too far for me to come if I suspect you're not."

"And I'll bring her," Ross added, putting his arm around Susanna. After a moment, he seemed to realize what he was doing, and withdrew it.

"Dad, I'm so glad you could be here!" Kelly exclaimed as she hugged him.

"I hope you have all the happiness there is in this world," Ross replied. "You deserve every bit of it."

"I'll tell you a secret," she whispered in his ear. "I don't deserve any of it."

"Well, have it your own way," he laughed in reply. "Just so you're happy: that's all that matters to me."

32
Good Works

"Hey Ross, hand me that nail gun, would you?"

Wiping his brow with one hand, Ross passed the requested tool up the ladder to Don Pillow with the other. Helping out with the "Jesus House" addition had seemed like a great idea when he had volunteered – but that was in the middle of an air-conditioned church meeting. He had forgotten two important things at that moment: the temperature of an average August day in Southern California, and that his twenty-something brain was stuck in the body of a fifty-something recovering stroke victim.

"Uh, Don, what do you say we... take five?" (What he actually wanted was closer to "forty-five," but he was too embarrassed to say so.) The indefatigable bricklayer good-naturedly agreed, and the two of them repaired to the shady side of the building, and the refreshment of the lemonade cooler.

"Seems like we're making pretty good progress," Ross observed, hoping to strike up a conversation that would stretch out the break.

"Yeah, I'd say it's going pretty well," Don agreed, capping the lemonade with a contented sigh. "But you should have seen the way this place looked when we started. It's amazing what the Lord has done in just a year."

Ross chuckled at that remark before he could catch himself, drawing a quizzical smile from Don.

"What? Did I say something funny?"

"Oh, nothing... don't mind me," said Ross with a wave of his hand. "It's just that I can't quite get used to all you guys talking like the Lord does everything personally. I mean, if He does it all Himself, why are we sweating out here in the heat, instead of sitting at home watching baseball?"

"Because He lets us be a part of his work," Don explained naturally, "so we can learn, and grow, and take pleasure in it along with Him."

"But if nobody gets any credit but God," Ross insisted, "then what's the point of trying harder? Didn't Jesus say He would reward every man according to his work?"

"I see you've been paying attention to the preaching," Don smiled. "And yes, He did say that. But the works that Jesus will reward aren't the ones we've accomplished by our own effort; they're works of faith, and faith is the gift of God. Even the Apostle Paul said he had 'obtained mercy of the Lord to be faithful.' So even if we love and obey Him all the rest of our lives, it's really just the result of his mercy."

"Which comes back to God getting all the credit again," Ross concluded with a wry smile. "Now don't get me wrong," he hastened to add, "I'm glad God is merciful. I'd be dead at least twice over if He weren't, and I'd never have gotten Susanna and Kelly back. But I'd still like to think I don't need... *just* mercy.

Surely I can do something to at least show Him I appreciate it."

"Absolutely," Don laughed. "You can take his free gift!"

Ross just smiled and shook his head. "That wasn't exactly what I had in mind."

Just then, a faint rumbling shook the ground, barely noticeable, but for a few loose nails rattling in the bottom of the tool carrier.

"Seems like we've been having more of those tremors lately," Ross remarked without alarm. (One didn't grow up in Southern California without getting used to earthquake tremors.) "Sure would be ironic if we got this thing all finished, and The Big One came along and knocked it flat."

"Well, God brought it through a fire," Don observed, "and I reckon He can handle an earthquake too. I mean, with our help, of course. I'll try to be on hand to hold up one wall, if you'll hold up the other!"

Ross raised an eyebrow.

"Just trying to go along with your strategy," Don grinned.

"Yeah, sure you are," Ross nodded facetiously.

The sound of tires squealing made both men turn in the direction of the street. Beth's Maverick, which looked like its driver must have lost her senses, lurched into the driveway, just barely missing the mailbox in the process. Once safely parked, Beth and Kelly emerged – the latter somewhat sheepishly, from the driver's side.

"Well, that explains some things," Don remarked drily. He gave an admiring tip of his hat to Beth. "O woman, great is thy faith!"

"By grace we have been saved," she replied, at least recovered enough from the scare to come up with an appropriate Scriptural rejoinder.

"At least I missed the mailbox," Kelly pointed out hopefully.

"Is that what you're planning to say to the state trooper on the driving exam?" Ross teased.

"I don't know," Kelly sighed. "All my friends have had their licenses for months, and I've flunked the test twice. Maybe I'll just wait and get my driver's license in Armenia. Which side of the road do they drive on over there, anyway?"

"Whichever side is still in one piece, I imagine," Don grimaced. "David says that between the breakup of the Soviet Union and the war they've had over there, their economy is a mess."

"Well, maybe we won't even need a car, then," Kelly said brightly.

"Ahem," Beth prompted, "getting back to the reason we're here...?"

"Oh, yeah," Kelly remembered, "there's been a change in plans. The chapel we had lined up to rent is going to be closed for renovations for the next two months, so we won't be able to have the wedding there after all."

"So, is it back to your church, then?" Ross asked. "An auto parts store isn't a very romantic venue for a storybook wedding."

"I wouldn't have cared," Kelly shrugged, "but Mom and Mrs. Nazarian both said it would never do. So we're going to move up to a church that David's family used to attend, called St. Simeon's, about ten miles out in the country. David says it's old, but really beautiful, with stained glass windows and everything. He told me to ask if he could borrow your truck this evening, so he can start hauling some things out there."

Ross pulled the keys out of his pocket, but held them midair for just a moment. "Promise me you won't try to drive it?"

"Promise," she said, and kissed him on the cheek. "Thanks, Dad. We have a few more errands to run, so we'd better get going."

Kelly turned to find that Beth had smoothly slipped around to the driver's seat. "Looks like I've been demoted again," she mourned.

"Keep trying," her dad admonished. "Kincaids never give up."

She flashed him another smile as she ducked into the passenger seat. Watching the car drive off (at a much saner speed than it had arrived) Ross couldn't help thinking about the day when Kelly's new husband and calling would take her away from him... again.

"I can't believe it's only three weeks away," he said to no one in particular. "It's like I just got here, and everyone's... leaving already."

"Life does have a way of slipping through our fingers," Don observed. "I know the kids that come to this clubhouse are sure going to miss your daughter.

But at least Beth will be here to keep the ministry going, and it sounds like Susanna's planning to be more involved, too."

"Yeah," Ross confirmed, "I still can't believe the school board actually created a position where she could work from home. They never had a substitute teacher coordinator before, so why do they need one now?"

"Well, I imagine they had their reasons," Don replied, "but God had his."

"Susanna seems to think it's so she can do this foster parenting thing," Ross said, without enthusiasm. "Now that I've showed her how to do the paperwork, she's all excited. She's convinced that this is her new ministry."

"But you aren't?"

"It's just that I don't see how she can handle another house full of kids at her age. Kristen is no trouble – she's actually a lot of help. But little kids are a different matter, especially without...." He paused. "Well, I guess there are just a few things where we aren't quite on the same page."

"There's an easy solution to that problem," Don encouraged. "You know what Book she's in, and I get the idea you already believe most of it."

"Yeah, I guess I do," Ross agreed. "But believing is one thing. Accepting, especially Susanna's way... well, that's something else. Anyway," he sighed, "I guess it's about time we got back to work."

33

Deja Vu

Chuck finished up the string of numbers on his calculator, hit the enter key, and noted the total with satisfaction. This month's profits were up over last year, even after the rent increase that came with his move to a better part of town, and hiring his first employee.

I wonder what Rocky Philips would say if he saw me now, Chuck thought with a smile. *Poor old Dave! Still slaving away in that nowhere job, trying to save enough money so he can go and be penniless on the other side of the world. He should have taken my offer when he had the chance.*

The strange thing about David and Kelly, though, was that they genuinely didn't seem to care about their economic prospects. All they could talk about, whenever he saw either of them, was how excited they were to be "going out to spread the Gospel." Mom wasn't making very good employment choices, either. This part-time "substitute coordinator" gig might keep food on the table, but that was about it. And foster parenting? You'd think she'd have had enough of that, the first time around.

But if there was one thing worse than his family's unconcern for their own financial future, it was the disregard they obviously had for his success. Not that they said anything dismissive, or stopped caring about him. But seriously, what did a fellow have to do to get noticed by these Christians? Walk out on his family for ten years, maybe? Come back under another name, and have a stroke? Maybe then they'd pay attention.

Spinning his chair around toward his wall calendar, Chuck marked off another day with a black X. Just three days to go until Kelly's wedding, and the rehearsal was tomorrow. Chuck wouldn't have thought of missing either, even though he knew Ross was going to be there too. Keeping contact with his mother and sister, without ever setting eyes on his father, had proven to be a task too complicated even for him to handle. Anyway, Chuck found it gave him some satisfaction to walk right past the man who had done the same to him so many years ago. He hoped he was giving him a taste of what it was like to have your existence totally ignored.

Chuck turned around at the sound of a couple of soft taps on his open office door.

"Anybody home?" Kelly asked teasingly, as she peered around the frame.

"Go away, I'm busy counting my money," Chuck replied in his best grouch voice. "Humbug to everything!"

"Humbug yourself, you young miser," Kelly laughed as she came in, and sat down in his creaky guest chair. "I see your office furniture is still broken."

"Yes, and I'm still driving my old VW, and the office windows are all filthy because I'm too cheap to pay anybody to clean them. Anything else you'd like to point out about my stinginess?"

"Just that you're going to kill yourself working eighty-hour weeks," his sister said pointedly. "Even though you don't go to church, you could at least take Sundays off. All the other garages do."

"Yeah, that's how I keep the edge on my competition," Chuck grinned. "I'll have plenty of time to relax when I've made my first million."

"No, after that you'll start working on your second million, and then your third, and then...."

"Yeah, yeah, I know," Chuck dismissed, "the *Treasure of Sierra Madre* principle. Well, I've got more sense than Humphrey Bogart, I should hope. When I get enough money, I plan to enjoy it."

"But how much is enough?" Kelly asked searchingly. "And how long do you expect you'll be able to enjoy it? Twenty years... maybe thirty?"

"My little sister, the fire-breathing evangelist." Chuck tried to cover up his irritation with an indulgent smile. "Better save your zeal for the mission field, Babe. You and that Armenian apostle of yours are going to need it. Speaking of which," he said, deliberately changing the subject, "what time did you say the rehearsal is tomorrow?"

"Four o'clock," she replied, sighing inwardly at the brick wall in her brother's heart. "But actually, Chuck, that's what I came over here to talk to you about."

"What, you need a few extra bucks for refreshments?"

"No...," she said slowly, obviously not eager to get into her subject. "But, there's a part of the ceremony that I thought we should talk about ahead of time. The part where you walk me down the aisle?"

Chuck nodded. They had never really discussed it, but he'd always assumed he'd be the one to give Kelly away, and she knew that.

"Wait a minute," he preempted, feeling his anger begin to rise, "you aren't thinking of having Ross...."

"I want both of you to walk with me," she explained, "one on each side. I've really prayed about this, Chuck, and with Dad there, it wouldn't be honoring him not to give him the chance...."

"And what about honoring me?" Chuck exploded. "Doesn't anybody care about how I feel? From the way you guys act, you'd think it was me that walked out on you and Mom twelve years ago!

"What kind of a father was he to you, Kelly? I'll tell you – a missing one! Absent without leave, over the wall when we needed him the most. What right does he have to give you away, when he never wanted you in the first place?"

"Chuck," Kelly pleaded, putting her hand on his arm, "please try to understand. I'm grateful for all you did, and I will always love you. But I love Jesus most of all, and He tells us to honor our parents – both of them – no matter what they did or didn't do for us. I have to obey Him, no matter what."

Chuck jerked his arm away from Kelly's grasp. "Well if Jesus is the one you love the most," he spat, "I'm sure you'd rather have him at your wedding than me. He and Ross can just walk you down the aisle together." He spun his chair back around, yanked open a file drawer, and began to sort through some papers that didn't need sorting. "I think you'd better go now," he said coldly.

Kelly said nothing for a long while. Chuck knew she was silently crying, but he didn't turn around. Slowly, she got up to leave, but paused in the door. "I love you, Chuck," she said hoarsely. "I know you may not believe that, but it's true. I love you, and Jesus loves you too. Don't keep shutting the door in his face. One day, you may find you can't get it open again."

"Suits me just fine," he replied cynically. "You can close it yourself, on your way out."

She went out, but she left the door open.

34
Everything That Can Be Shaken

St. Simeon's Church was about as picturesque a place as one could hope to find for the perfect wedding. Situated in the middle of an almond grove, it felt far away from the traffic and noise of the nearby city. The Armenian immigrants who had built it around the end of the nineteenth century, had given their small church all the dignified grace and beauty of an old-world cathedral, without making it unduly showy. The rays of the afternoon sun, slanting through the stained-glass windows, projected their rainbow hues onto the small group rehearsing the marriage ceremony near the front.

It's just like the song, Susanna mused. *That's how the Lord's life shines through us onto the people we meet every day. If only they could all see the colors like we do.*

Susanna's emotions were mixed on this happy day, when their closest friends and family had come together to help prepare for the wedding. Don and Tina Pillow were there, along with Hannah Wertheim, who had timed her latest visit to coincide with the wedding, and insisted on lending a hand in the culinary department. No one protested too much, however, since she was a superlative cook, and was quickly training her granddaughter to follow in her footsteps. Judging by the aromas arising from the basement kitchen, the dynamic duo was concocting something delicious for the meal that was planned after the rehearsal. Beth would be there too, though right now she was late for her role as maid of honor, probably held up in traffic.

The only one who would be conspicuously missing from the table this evening was Chuck. In some ways, Susanna felt as though she had traded her son for her husband. Chuck himself seemed determined to make that the equation, and although Susanna felt she was doing all she could in loving her son, and praying for him, her heart still ached with the loss. Her prayer, uttered on every thought of him, remained the same: *Whatever it takes, Lord, bring him home.*

One thing that boosted Susanna's faith was seeing how close to the Kingdom such prayers had brought the man she thought she would never see again. Ross had a few more steps left to walk through the narrow gate, but everyone in the fellowship seemed to think he wouldn't be long in coming.

Right now, he was happily busy with the sort of project he loved best. Aram Nazarian had borrowed an old, temperamental farm tractor from a friend, and brought it over to re-grade the driveway, in anticipation of an unusually large number of guests. The ungainly beast seemed disinclined to work so far from home, however, and defied the efforts of its unfamiliar operator to get it to start.

To Ross, however, the words "broken equipment" were like the starting bell to a thoroughbred, and he was soon up to his elbows in grease and disconnected parts, looking for the problem.

"They'll probably be out there half the night," Susanna joked to Meg Nazarian.

"Wouldn't be the first time for Aram," she agreed. "I think men really enjoy getting in over their heads with mechanical projects. It's always been a mystery to me what they see in them."

"I guess they probably say the same thing about us and our housecleaning binges," Susanna laughed. "Which reminds me, I guess we'd better get back down there and at least act like we're helping, before Hannah and Kristen have it all done."

As the two women descended the rather steep staircase, Susanna felt an unusually strong tremor move through the building. She reached for the railing to steady herself, but was alarmed to find it was shaking too. Something told her this was more than just a tremor, and it wasn't too hard to guess what might happen to an old building like this in a strong earthquake.

"Susanna, we'd better get outside," Meg suggested urgently, having to raise her voice now to be heard above the rumbling.

"Wait!" Susanna suddenly remembered. "We need to get Hannah and Kristen!" She took a step back down the stairs, and had the odd sensation that the world had begun moving in slow motion, as every detail suddenly came into sharp focus. The ring on

Meg's finger, the few strands of hair that had come loose as she tried to keep her balance on the stairs. Susanna felt herself falling, as helpless as a rag doll, sliding down the undulating staircase as the lights went out. *Jesus, please be with us,* was the only thought she could form, as it seemed the whole building came down on top of them.

Ross watched the unfolding horror from the parking lot, almost prostrate, unable to regain his footing on the crazily rolling ground. "Susanna!" he screamed. "Kelly!" He watched the venerable old church sway, and lean further, and further, as though reeling from each successive shock. Then, with a horrible, wrenching, creaking groan, it lost the battle and fell to its knees in an enormous cloud of dust.

It seemed to Ross as though the agonizing collapse had taken an hour, but in reality, it was all over in less than a minute. Almost choking on the dust that was still billowing from the ruin, he struggled to his feet and stumbled toward the wreckage. He was soon conscious of Aram alongside him, both of them calling out the names of their loved ones, as though they might somehow make them appear through the haze. *God, don't let me lose them now*, Ross prayed desperately in his mind. *Please let them be all right.*

As the dust began to settle, Ross and Aram realized they were facing a large part of the roof of the building, which was being held up on the opposite side by a section of wall that was still standing. The door was nowhere to be found, but inside, they could hear voices. "Someone is alive in there!" Ross exclaimed, gripping Aram's arm as a new hope surged through him.

Picking their way through broken glass and debris, the two men circled around to where the back door had been. That part of the wall was completely gone, but an opening remained, through which they could hear a voice they now recognized as David's. He was calling Kelly's name, with a desperate urgency in his voice that made Ross's blood run cold.

"David!" Aram shouted. "Are you guys okay in there?"

"I... I don't know," came the uncertain answer. "I can't find Kelly!"

"Tina and I are all right," Don Pillow called out. "But my legs are pinned. Is there any way you can get in and help us?" Aram tried the opening, but found it too small, and Ross knew it wouldn't work for him either. Just then they heard running footsteps in the broken glass, and turned to find Beth, her face ashen and streaked with tears.

"Did everybody get out?" she asked fearfully.

"I've got a mobile phone in my truck," Ross replied, not answering her question. "Make sure somebody is sending help."

"I can take care of that," Aram volunteered. "I think Beth might be able to squeeze through that opening."

"We don't know if the wreckage is stable," Ross warned, but Beth was already climbing in. She reappeared a few moments later, and grabbed the flashlight and first aid kit Aram had brought from the truck. "There's sort of a cave inside there," she explained. "I think the structure they built underneath the steeple is what's holding it up."

"Even if she can get to everybody," Ross reasoned, "no one else but Kelly could fit through that opening."

"Ross," Don called, "are the tools we used on the addition still in the back of your truck?"

"Yes – the battery powered saw!" Ross exclaimed. Within a few minutes, he and Aram had enlarged the hole, and were able to join Beth inside the cramped, dusty space. After some work, they managed to free Don's legs, and Aram carried him outside, with some help from a slightly dazed Tina.

"Ross!" they heard David yell. "I found Kelly! She's unconscious, but she's still breathing!"

Fighting their way through the wreckage, and praying they wouldn't bring it down on their heads, Ross and Beth made their way toward the sound of David's voice. They found him holding Kelly, who lay senseless in his arms, with an ugly gash on her head.

"She's alive," David repeated, "but we've got to get her to the hospital fast; she may have a skull fracture. I'm afraid Pastor Grayson didn't make it." He nodded sadly toward the still form of their faithful shepherd. "The same beam fell on them both, and he tried to protect her. I had just stepped away for a minute...."

"There's no time for that now, David," Ross said, a little more shortly than he intended. "I'm sorry about Pastor Grayson," he added in a gentler tone, "but we need to save the ones we can. Do you know where your mom and Susanna are?"

"In the basement, I hope," David said. "Don was trying to get to them when the roof came down." Ross breathed a sigh of relief. Their chances were a lot better down there – provided that none of the floor had collapsed.

Slowly, the three of them maneuvered the unconscious Kelly back out to the opening. "Where are those stupid emergency workers?" Ross fumed. "What good does it do to even have a 911 service?"

"The dispatcher said they've been swamped with calls," Aram explained. "Apparently the damage in the city was extensive, and they've had to close some of the bridges."

Beth was quickly selected as the obvious choice to drive Kelly, Don, and Tina to the hospital. As much as David wanted to help with the rescue efforts, he couldn't even stand on what was probably a fractured ankle, so he agreed to go with Kelly instead.

Once the makeshift ambulance was loaded and sent on its way, Ross and Aram crawled back into the wreckage to try and find a way into the basement. They finally located the stairwell, but found it completely blocked by a large section of the concrete foundation wall.

"Susanna?" Ross shouted as loudly as he could. "Meg? Are you guys down there?"

"Is that you, Ross?" a feeble voice called up.

"It's Meg," Aram said, the relief evident in his voice. "Are you okay, honey?"

"I'm all right," she replied, "and so is Kristen. Susanna is bleeding really badly, though, and we don't know what's wrong with Mrs. Wertheim – she's not responsive. Can you get us out?"

"Hold on, sweetheart," he replied, "we're trying!"

"This wall section is way too heavy to lift," Ross concluded after trying to budge it. "Could we cut a hole in the floor instead, and reach them that way?"

Aram shook his head. "Oak boards. I burned up more than one saw blade on them when I helped put air conditioning in this church years ago.

"Well, we've got to get them out somehow!" Ross almost shouted, feeling the panic mounting inside him. "Susanna could bleed to death by the time the rescue crews get here."

The two men looked at each other, and then remembered at the same time.

"The tractor!"

35
Mirror, Mirror

Hearing the car behind him honk its horn, Chuck reflexively honked at the guy in front of him. Both drivers knew it was pointless – they might be within sight of the hospital, but it would probably take another hour to get there, no matter how hard anyone laid on their horn.

Chuck never could have imagined finding himself trapped in such a nightmare. At first he had thought he was lucky, when the shaking stopped, and his shop had only suffered minor damage. But when he saw on TV that the epicenter of the earthquake was near the church, he started to worry. *They said that building was old – what if it fell down on top of them?*

The thought struck him with a chill, as he remembered his last conversation with Kelly. He almost jumped in his car right then, but changed his mind and decided to stay near the phone. When it rang, he tried to believe that the news would be good. But it was Beth's voice on the other end, and he could tell she'd been crying.

Chuck listened in disbelief as his worst fears materialized, and Beth told him the church had indeed collapsed, with almost everyone inside. Kelly was in critical condition, and might not live through the night.

"Can you get to the hospital?" she pleaded.

"I'll get there if I have to walk!" he heard himself promise, though his mind was still reeling from the shock. With a surge of fear, he realized that Beth hadn't mentioned his mother.

"What about Mom, Beth? And the others, are they okay?"

"Pastor Grayson was killed," she replied, obviously struggling to hold herself together. "They think your mom and some of the other ladies may be trapped in the basement. But don't try to go out there: there's a bridge partly collapsed on the main route, and they'll only let emergency traffic go the other way."

Fifteen minutes later, Chuck was sitting in the middle of the worst traffic jam he had ever seen. *Forget about getting out to the church*, Chuck thought angrily. *I can't even move six blocks in this mess!* Disgusted, he parked his VW on the shoulder, got out, and started walking.

God, he thought accusingly, *how could you let this happen? Aren't they supposed to be your children?*

But even while his heart was pointing the finger at God, Chuck knew there was a far more convincing and accusing finger pointing back at him. Kelly might die tonight – she might be dead already. And the last words he'd said to her? *Close the door on your way out.*

Those words, in all their mocking, stinging sarcasm, jabbed at his heart again and again. He was supposed to be the good big brother, the faithful protector. And yet, where was he when Kelly had really needed him? He had brushed her aside, just like....

Unwilling to face that thought, Chuck broke into a run, his sneakers pounding the hot sidewalk, as though he could somehow escape the guilt and condemnation that were pressing in on him. At last he made it to the crowded emergency room, sweating and out of breath. He scanned the crowd of worried and tearful faces, and finally caught sight of Beth. He went over and sat down beside her, laying what was supposed to be a reassuring hand on her arm.

"We'll get through this," he said, with a certainty he did not feel.

"How do you know, Chuck?" she asked, the sincerity of the unexpected question shining through her tears. "Just what are you trusting in? The doctors say Kelly has maybe a fifty-fifty chance to pull through."

"Well, what do you want me to say?" he shot back. "That I'm sorry, that I should have been there? Okay, I'm sorry – I acted like a jerk. I know she probably told you what I said."

"No, she didn't," Beth said quietly, "but I can imagine."

"Look," he said more quietly, "I really am sorry – sorrier than you can possibly imagine. If Kelly doesn't make it, I don't think I'll ever forgive myself. I'd like to... that is... would you pray with me?"

Beth hesitated. "I'll be happy to pray *for* you, Chuck, but I can't pray *with* you unless something has changed since the last time we spoke. God won't listen to someone who comes with unforgiveness in their heart."

"Why does everything have to come back to me and my dad?" he sputtered angrily. "It's easy for other people to say, 'well, you should just forgive.' But they haven't stood in my shoes, or tried living my life. Beth, if you had been there that day, and seen the way he just walked out on us...."

Even as he said the words, Chuck's mind went back to the day his mother had told him who Roger Morton really was. Hadn't he refused to listen, and walked out on her just the same way? And then, there was the inescapable image of the way he had rebuffed Kelly in the office, and ignored her tears....

Just like his father had.

"I'm just like him," he said aloud. Four true words, obvious to the whole world, except the one man who refused to look in the mirror and acknowledge them. "All these years I've hated him, and all the time, I was becoming more like him every day." He shook his head slowly in disbelief. "How is it possible to fool yourself like that?"

"It's easy, Chuck," Beth replied. "You just walk in darkness. The Bible says that when you do that, you don't know where you're going. You can plan to end up in one place, and find yourself at the very opposite end of the universe. But that's not where God wants you to be. He wants you to live in the light, to know where you're going – and Who is going to take you there."

She reached over and took his hand again. "I'd like to pray for you now, if you'll let me."

"Pray for all you're worth, Beth," he said, squeezing her hand tightly. "Pray for all of us."

36

Just Mercy

Ross and Aram scrambled as quickly as they could out of the collapsed building, both their minds on that partly-repaired tractor engine. Just before the earthquake hit, Ross had located the problem, and borrowed a part off his truck that he thought might fix it.

Just as they emerged, an ambulance careened into the church parking lot, sirens wailing. Aram explained the situation to the two EMT's, while Ross worked feverishly to get the engine back together. Finally, he managed to get it started – but just barely.

"It's missing on one cylinder... maybe two," Ross yelled to the others. "But it just might do the job anyway." Slowly, he willed the recalcitrant machine around to the far side of the church, where they quickly hooked a pair of tow chains to exposed pieces of rebar in the collapsed wall.

Now under load, the engine strained and groaned, but the beast began to move, and the wall with it. Then suddenly, with a stutter and a wheeze, the motor died.

"No!" Ross shouted, pounding the steering wheel in frustration. He turned the key again and again, but to no avail.

"Just another foot," one of the medics observed, "and gravity would do the rest."

Ross realized the man was right – the tractor had stopped just short of a steep incline. If they could somehow make it top the crest, its own weight should be enough to lift the wall. Quickly, he switched the gear to neutral, and climbed out of the operator's seat.

"Come on, guys, let's push it over the edge!" All four men got behind the machine and pushed with every ounce of strength they could muster, but the ground was soft, and the futility of their efforts soon became obvious. Nothing was going to budge that three-ton beast the last twelve inches.

Down in that basement, Susanna's life was ebbing away, and there was nothing in the world that a man named Ross Kincaid could do about it. Feeling, for the first time in his life, his own utter helplessness, Ross fell to his knees and cried.

"God, I can't do it!" he prayed in desperation. "I know I don't deserve your mercy, but I'm ready to ask for it anyway. Please... *just mercy*."

For a few seconds, there was silence. Then, another deep tremor began to shake the ground.

"Get away from the building," one of the medics warned. "The aftershock could bring the rest of it down!"

But it didn't. Instead, it shifted the ground under the tractor so that it began to roll – over the edge and down the slope, raising the wall the few precious feet they needed for the rescue.

Within a few minutes, the EMT's brought up Mrs. Wertheim, who was unconscious, and very gray. The medics said she'd had a heart attack, and from their demeanor, Ross guessed her chances weren't good. Susanna had lost a lot of blood, but managed a wan smile as Ross took her hand.

"Is everyone okay?" she asked weakly. "Kelly, and David?"

"They're alive, honey," was all that Ross could honestly assure her, as he climbed into the ambulance. Kristen asked to stay with her grandmother, and soon they were all speeding back toward the city. When the EMT had done all he could for both patients, he paused long enough to look at Ross with amazement.

"I have never seen anything like that aftershock moving the wall," he said. "Somebody up there must have been looking out for you guys."

"Not just somebody," Ross corrected. "Jesus."

Susanna opened her eyes and smiled. "Amen," she whispered softly.

The ambulance ride was a long one, as the nearest hospital, where Beth had taken her load of passengers, was already full. Conditions at the next closest hospital, when they finally arrived, were about what one would expect with a disaster the size of the recent earthquake. The triage nurse seemed confident that Susanna would be all right; although her injuries included several broken ribs, a broken arm, and a dislocated shoulder, they had managed to stop the bleeding in time.

When it came to Hannah, however, the nurse just shook her head and scribbled something on the chart. Without time to consider hiding the truth from Kristen, Ross simply asked the nurse what she had written.

"We'll keep her comfortable," she said, "but I'm afraid there's not much more we can do. Her body is already shutting down."

"Could you put her in the room with Susanna?" Ross asked. "I know she would appreciate it."

The nurse merely nodded her assent to the orderly. When both Susanna and Mrs. Wertheim were settled, Ross left for the other hospital, to try and check on Kelly. Kristen, who had said nothing the whole time, resumed her place by her grandmother's side in the hospital room.

"Kristen, honey," Susanna asked softly, "are you okay?"

"No," the girl answered honestly, "not really. Why do things like this have to happen, Mrs. Kincaid? Why would God have to take her away, just when I was getting to know her?" She brushed away the tears, and held tightly to her grandmother's hand.

"I don't know the answer to that, Kristen," Susanna replied, with equal frankness. "Sometimes we don't get the 'why's' answered in this life. But we always know the 'who,' and that's Jesus. He holds us, even when it hurts, and He's promised that his plans for us are good, even when it looks like everything's falling apart."

The two of them sat in silence throughout the evening, as the sun slowly set. Ross had promised to try and get in touch with Henry, but with conditions in the city, it seemed unlikely that he would be able to make it in time. As the last rays of daylight faded from the curtains, Hannah suddenly, briefly opened her eyes and looked at her granddaughter.

"*Meydele*," she whispered, "always love God." Then, with a look that seemed to see Someone they could not, she softly spoke one more word: "*Mashiach.*" Then, peacefully, she closed her eyes, and breathed her last.

"What does it mean?" Susanna asked.

Kristen turned toward her, eyes glistening with tears. "It means 'Messiah.'"

37
Truth And Consequences

The touch of a hand on his shoulder was enough to rouse Chuck from a tense, fitful sleep. In the dark, he couldn't see who it was, but the figure motioned him to follow, so he did. Carefully, they stepped around the army cots that had been placed almost wall-to-wall in the temporary Red Cross shelter, next door to the hospital. Squinting in the bright light of the corridor, Chuck recognized the pale, drawn face of his father.

"I knew you'd want to hear the news right away, Chuck," Ross said. "They just told me that Kelly's going to make it."

Chuck sank down on a bench, leaned against the wall, and exhaled his relief. "Thank you, God," he whispered – perhaps the first sincere words he'd spoken to his Creator in his entire life.

"Mind if I... sit down and talk to you for a minute?" Ross asked hesitantly. "You don't have to say anything – you don't even have to listen. But I'd like to get a few things said, anyhow."

Chuck just nodded.

"Years ago," Ross began, "when you were a little boy, I took you up for a ride in my airplane. It was the only time I ever did that, because I heard plenty about it from your mom later. But I remember how much you wanted to fly the plane, and when I took my hands off yours, you really thought you were doing it. 'I'm flying all by myself!' you said."

"I remember that... sort of," Chuck recalled quietly.

"Well, I just laughed," Ross continued, "but the truth is, you were really giving me a picture of myself. All my life I've wanted, more than anything else, to be in control, and independent... to be free. Money gave me that freedom for a while, but a wife and kids were too much restraint. That's the real reason I left, because I felt like I was losing control.

"When I finally realized that I wanted to try and make things right with you guys, it still had to be on my terms. I thought that by coming back as a different person, I could show you all how much I'd changed, without risking your rejection. Even after that scheme fell apart, I still thought I could do enough good to *deserve* a second chance. I still wanted to be the one in the pilot's seat.

"But today, I came face to face with the fact that I have no control, over anything. You might have heard that I got your mom out of that church basement, but I didn't – God did. I could have had all the money, and all the influence in the world at that moment, and it wouldn't have moved that concrete slab one single inch. It was nothing but his mercy, just like every good thing that's ever come my way. He never really let go of the controls, even when I literally crashed the plane. All the time when I thought I was flying, it was just his grace, holding me up.

"There's nothing I can ever do to make up for what I did to you, and your Mom, and Kelly. I can't turn back time, and undo the pain and heartbreak. I can't give you back the childhood you missed out on because a proud, stubborn, willful man, that you didn't choose to be your father, walked out on his responsibility. There's no way I can make you forget that, or give you any reason why you should. I don't deserve forgiveness; I can't buy it, finagle it, or demand it. But there's one thing I can do, and that's ask for it."

Ross leaned forward, and looked earnestly into his son's eyes. "And Chuck," he said hoarsely, "that's what I'm doing right now. Will you... forgive me?"

Many times over the years, Chuck had pictured an eventual encounter with his father. He had imagined all the hateful, vengeful things he'd say, the poisoned darts he'd fling at the man who had once wounded him so deeply.

But now, suddenly, none of that seemed to make sense. This man that he had hated and despised, the supposed source of everything that had gone wrong with his life: he was really just a picture of Chuck himself. To refuse to forgive him would be like saying he didn't want mercy for himself either. He might not be quite ready to open that door, but despite what he'd said to Kelly, he didn't really want to close it forever, either.

"Dad," he started – and suddenly his voice stuck in his throat. So many years, so many heartaches since he last used that word. He swallowed hard.

"I may not be able to forget," he tried again, "but I... do... forgive you."

Ross let out a long, slow sigh, and closed his eyes. "Thank you, Chuck. You don't know how much that means to me."

But in a strange way, those words really meant more to Chuck than they did to his father. It was like popping the cap off a soda bottle that someone had been shaking for twelve years. All the emotions that he'd pent up for half his life: the fear, insecurity, bitterness, and anger, were about to spill out, and he knew he couldn't contain them. Without another word, he got up, left the building, and walked out into the darkened streets of the city. And as he walked, he cried.

38

Here Comes The Bride

Carefully adjusting the sling that held her cast, Susanna settled into a folding chair on the front row, and resigned herself to a spectator's role in the wedding preparations for her daughter. It seemed that anytime she tried to lift a finger to help with anything, she was quickly chased off, fussed over, and told she should be resting. The experience was reminiscent of her first pregnancy, Susanna thought with a smile – except that now, the people who surrounded her really, truly cared.

Even Pastor Grayson's widow, who had only had a few weeks to recover from the shock and sorrow of his unexpected home-going, laid aside her own grief to help make this a joyful occasion. The small group had laid their dear pastor to rest the week after the earthquake, and although no vote was taken, everyone knew that it would be Don Pillow who would take his place. In today's ceremony, he would use Pastor Grayson's Bible, found clutched in his hand in death, as it so often had been during his life.

As many of the church members as were able, had also accompanied Kristen to the traditional Jewish burial service for her grandmother. But knowing, as they did, the faith in Jesus she had found before her death, the church held their own private memorial service to celebrate her entry into eternal life, as well.

Although David and Kelly's departure for Armenia had been delayed until next spring, to give her plenty of time to recuperate, neither of them wanted to put off the wedding a day longer than they had to. David, in fact, wanted to have the marriage in Kelly's hospital room. Kelly would no doubt have agreed in a heartbeat, but being still in a coma at the time, she was not consulted, and more traditional, sensible views prevailed.

The site chosen for the wedding, though it might have seemed strange to some, was the very same ground upon which it had been originally scheduled to take place. The congregation of St. Simeon's, many of whom no longer lived close by, had elected to relocate, instead of rebuilding on the same spot. They had the rubble cleared away, the basement filled in, and a small gazebo erected, to serve as a memorial of their church, and those who had fallen along with it.

When they heard what the church had done, David and Kelly were each separately impressed that this gazebo was the only proper place to exchange their vows. It was there that God had spared their lives, and there they would return to show that, through Jesus Christ, love triumphs over death.

Looking back over the many happy faces among the congregation as they found their seats, Susanna saw one that she didn't recognize. A slightly stooped, and rather careworn-looking old man stood alone near the very back of the crowd. Kristen, who was sitting next to Susanna, spotted him at the same time she did, and immediately jumped up and ran toward him with a little cry of joy. Taking his hand, she led the reluctant old gentleman up front to meet Susanna.

"This is my granddad," she said proudly. "Grandad, I want you to meet Mrs. Kincaid."

"Confidentially," she added, "I call her 'mom,' which sort of makes you related, I guess. You don't mind, do you?"

Henry Wertheim shook his head, with just the slightest hint of a smile. "Mrs. Kincaid," he said, "I want to personally thank you for all you've done for Kristen, and for the hospitality you showed to my wife Hannah, as well."

"Your wife was a very special lady," Susanna replied sincerely, "and as much of a blessing to us as Kristen continues to be. I am so sorry for your loss."

"She has found her rest," Henry nodded with resignation, "and I must find a way to go on without her." In his voice, Susanna could hear the same aching loneliness she knew so well from the years before she met Jesus.

"I hope, Mrs. Kincaid..." Henry continued hesitantly, "I hope that you might allow Kristen to come and visit me from time to time."

"As often as she likes," Susanna affirmed. "And Mr. Wertheim, the door to our house is always open. You can come whenever you like, and stay as long as you like. Even though we're not from Abraham's original tree, we love God's Chosen People. And on top of that, like Kristen said, we're sort of related."

Somewhat embarrassed by this heartfelt invitation, the elderly Jew murmured his thanks, and found a seat with Kristen a few rows back. Tina began the prelude on a piano brought out for the occasion, and the wedding ceremony commenced.

At length, Kelly appeared, wearing Susanna's wedding dress, and looking every bit the joyful, radiant bride. Chuck took her arm and walked her down the rose-strewn aisle. When he reached the spot where his dad stood waiting, he kissed Kelly on the cheek, and took his seat next to Susanna. Ross, still limping just slightly, escorted his daughter up to the gazebo, where her bridegroom stood waiting. In his eyes, no one else was there.

Pastor Don asked Ross the age-old question: "Who gives this woman in marriage to this man?"

Ross hesitated a moment, and then broke from the script. "Her Father," he said. "And her mother, and her brother... and I." Smiling through tears, Kelly kissed her dad, and took the hand of her soon-to-be husband.

As Susanna watched her daughter take the solemn vows of marriage, she couldn't help but remember that evening so long ago when she had said the same words. The same – and yet so different. Because when Kelly promised to love and cherish her husband, in sickness and in health, it was with Jesus' love filling her heart. When David slipped the ring on her finger, and vowed it would be "until death do us part," he was relying only on the faithfulness of the One who always keeps his word.

And in the joy of this holy union, there was a reminder of the hope yet to come. One day, the Bride of Christ would be joined to her Bridegroom, and feel his loving hand wipe all her tears away, forever. No matter how dark the night, or how deep the sorrow, His promise would always remain, like the first glow of dawn on a far horizon.

"Blessed are you that weep now... for you shall laugh."